I0571392

Second String

The String Serial
Part Two

Andrea Ring

Originally published in 2016 by Square Gorilla Press. For information, visit http://www.squaregorilla.com.

ISBN 978-0692730416

Cover image:

Copyright © 2016 Michael Ring

Cover design:

Hannah Reams, http://www.hannahreams.com

Change is necessary.

"Three men since I've started seeing you," I say, "and three strikeouts. Being social hasn't gotten me anywhere."

"Is that how you see it?" he asks.

I shrug. "On the relationship front."

"I can name five benefits of your sociability off the top of my head," he says. "Name two."

One springs easily to mind. "I'm not really pining after Matt anymore."

He nods in agreement, waiting for me to continue.

"And I'm able to play music again."

Nod. Stare. A little more nodding.

"And...I'm owning who I am more. I mean, I can voice my opinions. And I actually went out on a blind date, without my guitar, and I had a good time. I contributed to the conversation and got to know the guy." I smile in triumph. *See, Dr. Steinburg? I'm learning.*

Dedication

To my mom, who read *First String* and said, "You did get a little serious, but it's good. Keep going."

Acknowledgements

To my talented cover artist, Hannah Reams, thank you for your patience!

Chapter 1

I call in sick to work and drive to my mother's. She's sipping coffee in her yoga pants, gearing up for an early-morning class.

"Did you get fired?" she asks as she pecks my cheek and moves to the kitchen.

"Why would you think I got fired?"

She pours me a cup of coffee. "It's a Monday morning and you're supposed to be at work. Was there a gas leak?"

I sigh and sip my coffee. "I called in sick. We have a huge problem with Mayberry & Foster." My mother gives me a blank stare. "Mayberry & Foster. The firm that handles Dad's music rights?"

"Oh." She goes back to her place on the couch, and I follow her. "What problem is that?"

"Did you agree to let Dad's songs be used in that video game?"

"We signed to that hero game. The one where you play along with the fake guitar with those rainbow buttons."

"Not that one," I say. "It's called *Cop Killer Reloaded*."

"*Cop Killer*?" she says with a grimace. "That game is sick. No."

"What about Senator Horton's campaign? Did you know about that?"

She swallows her coffee. "You can't get worked up about all these inquires, Hope. Our attorneys bring us the deals, and we agree or not. It's not Mayberry's fault some jackass wants the songs."

"I'm not worked up about inquires," I say. "So they brought the Horton thing to you. And you turned them down?"

"Of course I did," she says. "Don't tell me you think we should do it."

I shake my head. "It's done. I ran into one of our attorneys last night, and he didn't know who I was. He let it slip that he closed both the Spotify deal and the Horton campaign deal for us. And Dad's songs have been in that *Cop Killer* game for a year."

She pales. "That's not possible. And you and I discussed the subscription service deals, and we decided against them. I had a very pointed conversation with them about it."

"Is it possible you signed something you shouldn't have?" I ask. "I mean, I don't know how they expect to get away with this. These are three very visible deals. They couldn't expect to hide them from us forever."

"It's possible," she finally admits. "I never signed your name, though. I wouldn't do that."

I rise. "I need to hire a new attorney, just for this. And then we need someone else to represent Dad's catalog."

"I can't believe this," she says. "These are attorneys! They're supposed to follow the law."

I just laugh. "Ironic, isn't it?"

Chapter 2

I drive home after dinner. My mother and I found an attorney to sick on Mayberry, and we managed to meet with her, retain her, and get the ball rolling. I'm looking forward to a hot bubble bath and eight hours of sleep.

Several cars are parked around my house when I pull into the driveway. I step out of the car, and I notice a woman in a suit get out of hers.

"Ms. Cruz?" she calls.

I close my door. "Yes."

"Penelope Capshaw with *Entertainment Now*," she says, jogging over to me. "Can I ask you a few questions?"

I'm totally caught off guard. "Uh, I don't think—"

"Can you tell us why you visited with an attorney today?"

I rear my head back. "That's none of your business."

"Does it have to do with your father?"

I push past her and head to my door. But she follows.

"Do you have plans to release an album?"

I unlock my door and turn on her. "You're on my property. Please leave."

And I shut the door in her face.

⅋

I lock the door tight. Then I go to every window and door, closing shades and curtains, ensuring they're all locked. This is downright creepy.

After ten minutes, I peek through the side of the front curtain. The cars are still there, and Miss Penelope seems to be doing a TV spot, with a camera on her and a microphone at her lips. Christ.

I don't know the protocol on this. Are they allowed to just stand in my front yard? In the street? Can I call the police? Should I call the police?

I decide to ignore them for the moment. If they hang out on the property, then I'll make a phone call. Otherwise, I'll probably just get more unwanted attention.

Matt, my ex-husband, calls while I'm in the bath.

"I just wanted to thank you again," he says. "The vet called me today. I can pick up Strings in the morning."

"Glad she's recovering," I say. That poor puppy, Strings. When Matt had an emergency in the middle of the night and asked me to watch her, I left her alone on the floor of my bedroom, and she managed to swallow part of a tampon that was in my jeans pocket. The vet had to cut it out of her.

"I asked the vet about the bill. She said you paid it."

I sigh. "Let it go. Strings is fine."

"I can't let $3,000 go!" he says. "It's a lot of money. Let me make payments."

I have the money and Matt doesn't. Not that I'd point this out to him.

"It's my fault," I say. "I dropped the ball. Moving on."

"When did you get so stubborn?" Matt says. "I don't remember you being this way."

"I thought you wanted me to have a little backbone," I say. "Isn't that part of the reason you left?"

He sighs. "Classic case of not knowing how good I had it. Or maybe that getting what you want never turns out how you think it will."

"My stubbornness will never affect you again," I say. "We're divorced. There's no reason for us to ever speak again."

Matt is silent.

"Matt?"

"Yeah, uh, I should go."

"Kiss Strings for me," I say.

"Will do."

And he hangs up.

Chapter 3

Dr. Steinburg listens patiently as I tell him about our problem with our attorneys at Mayberry & Foster.

But he doesn't seem that interested. He wants to know how I've been progressing personally.

"I bought a book on how to knit," I say. "My best friend's pregnant, and I thought it would be fun to knit things for the baby."

He tries to hide a smile. "While that's a great thing to do in your spare time, it's not very social."

"Three men since I've started seeing you," I say, "and three strikeouts. Being social hasn't gotten me anywhere."

"Is that how you see it?" he asks.

I shrug. "On the relationship front."

"I can name five benefits of your sociability off the top of my head," he says. "Name two."

One springs easily to mind. "I'm not really pining after Matt anymore."

He nods in agreement, waiting for me to continue.

"And I'm able to play music again."

Nod. Stare. A little more nodding.

"And...I'm owning who I am more. I mean, I can voice my opinions. And I actually went out on a blind date, without my guitar, and I had a good time. I contributed to the conversation and got to know the guy." I smile in triumph. *See, Dr. Steinburg? I'm learning.*

He smiles back.

"How's your relationship with your mother?"

"Fine," I say. "She told me that you've had her sleeping with my baby blanket. As a reminder that she didn't do everything wrong."

Nod.

"And with this legal crap we're going through...it made me realize I need to take responsibility for my own life more. She's the one who's handled my dad's estate, mostly, and I let her, because it made her feel like she was taking care of me. But the truth is...he left everything to me. An attorney had power until I turned eighteen, and then, when I did, I gave Mom the power to continue making decisions, but that was because I still couldn't face much associated with my dad. It's long past time I faced it."

"He left everything to you? Everything?"

I nod. "I hated him for that, because I know a part of my mom resented it. I mean, how could she not?"

"Your mother never told me this," Dr. Steinburg says. "I strongly feel that if it had bothered her, she would have said something to me."

I shrug. "Who knows what goes on in her head? It's one of the few things Matt actually fought with me about."

"How so?"

"He thought I should give Mom their house. Sign the deed over to her, I mean. And it's not that I didn't want her to have it—I certainly don't want it—but I just couldn't face all the legal stuff. And I was pretty sure she wouldn't take it."

"She's living there now, right?"

I nod.

"I'm not going to try to persuade you one way or the other," he says, "but you realize this creates a difficult power dynamic between you two?"

I nod again. "I know. She's at my mercy. If I decided to screw her over, I could. I could evict her from the house, or stop paying her monthly royalties—"

"Wait. Your mother is completely dependent upon you for her finances?"

"I'm sure she has money saved," I say. "She makes, like, $50,000 a month."

Dr. Steinburg frowns. "And you're okay with that?"

My eyes sting. "My dad set things up this way because my mom was a bigger mess than I was. He didn't want me to have to rely on her."

"And he knew you'd take care of her," he finishes.

I nod.

"You know, your mother is not a mess anymore. She's stable, and she's capable. It's your choice, but I think you should think about separating your finances. I would say the same to any parent whose adult child were dependent on them. You cannot have an equal relationship with that kind of concentrated power."

I nod again.

"Just think about it."

Chapter 4

Martika invites me over for dinner. As soon as I walk in the door, she waves me over to her computer.

"Take a look at this," she says.

I'm looking at the *Cupid's Lair* website, and a profile of…me.

"What did you do?" I say.

"I created a profile for you," she says. "Read it. Tell me what you think."

"Martika."

"Just read it."

So I read aloud: "Single and sweet musician/writer looking for that special loyal guy to share music, memories, and passionate nights. I enjoy baseball, rock climbing, playing guitar, and cooking dinner for my man. I prefer boxers to briefs, open my presents Christmas morning, and hate rude people. I'm looking for someone active, fit, intelligent, and well-read. Cowboys, especially, should contact me."

She laughs, and I raise an eyebrow at her. "Seriously?"

"You can tweak it," she says. "That was just off the top of my head."

I close her laptop with a click. "No way. I'm not writing some ridiculous singles ad."

She opens the computer back up, totally unfazed. "Something like 10,000 couples a day get married from this site," she says. "Those are great odds."

"You actually believe that?"

"Ben and I met online," she says. "You know that."

"But you were both in the military," I say. "Neither of you had many options when you were deployed."

"You can't dismiss this," she says. "Tons of people meet this way. And it's totally secret. You can just browse your matches, and no one knows. If none of them interests you, then fine. No harm, no foul."

"With my luck, I won't get any matches," I say.

She nudges me. "Come on. Just tweak the ad and hit send. It'll give you matches right away, based on the questionnaire I filled out. Let's just see."

"I'm not contacting any of them," I say.

"Fine."

We work on my blurb for over an hour. What a waste of time. Martika reads the final product:

"Musician/writer looking for loyalty, honesty, and trust. I love to play my guitar, cook for my friends, and take care of my family. What you look like, how much money you make—not important. I want to be with a nice guy, be treated well, and give the same to him."

I nod once. Sounds good to me.

Martika sighs. "It's you. And it's honest. Let's just hope the lack of marketing pizazz doesn't hurt you."

I roll my eyes.

If a guy is looking for pizazz…yeah. Probably best to look elsewhere.

છ

I hit send.

The computer churns. And returns 75 matches.

Martika squeals. "See? I told you!"

Huh. I start scrolling through them.

"Wait. Stop! That guy is gorgeous."

"It says he's Mormon and that faith is important to him," I point out. "I'm not gonna try to convert a sexy Mormon."

"What would you convert him to?"

"Nothing," I say. "That's the point. It's important to him. Why would I waste his time?"

"Because he's hot."

"Why would he even show up in my search?" I ask. "Isn't religion an important factor?"

"Oh," she says. "I put that you're Catholic. Maybe that's why."

"My parents were Catholic," I say. "Not me."

"You were baptized," she says. "You had your First Communion."

"Stop hassling me," I say. "I don't practice, and you know it."

"Why is that?"

I glare at her. "I refuse to be like him. My dad actually carried rosary beads in his pocket every day of his life. What a fucking hypocrite."

Martika looks at me. "I'm sensing some hostility."

I laugh. "You think?"

"You know...religion and spirituality, they're personal. There are plenty of people from every religion who are hypocrites or jerks or outright murderers. That has nothing to do with your personal faith."

"Can we please table this discussion? We're supposed to be looking for hot guys."

"I thought you wanted a nice guy, not a hot guy."

I sigh, and we go back to scrolling.

"How about him?" Martika says. "Fourth-generation almond farmer. I didn't know almond farms were a thing. He looks fit. And farmers are hard workers. You like almonds."

"He's two hours away," I say. "Next."

We scroll past mustache guy, dirty guy, lives-with-his-mother guy.

"Here's an interesting one," she says. "'Divorced with three kids. Looking for an equal partner, someone independent, fun, and drama-free. I want to grow old with someone and share the important things.'"

I look at the picture. Distinguished, in a nice suit, bold emerald tie. Hair going silver, but in that hot Sean Connery way.

"Says he's 45," I say. "Do you think that's too old? And I want kids of my own. He already has some."

Martika looks at me. "You're interested."

I shrug. "I like the equal partner thing. And maybe he's pretty set in his life since he's older. I like the idea of not having to coddle someone."

"He's in Newport Beach," she says. "Message him. You have nothing to lose."

She's right. I have nothing to lose. So I type a brief message and send it.

Chapter 5

I meet with Mr. Alec Chang at his office in the Orange City Centre. I didn't tell him who I was, or give him any details when I made the appointment. I was afraid someone in his office would let it slip to the press.

Paranoid is me.

But I'm impressed that I get a cappuccino before I can even sit, and that I'm treated well by his staff despite being fairly young. I appreciate being taken seriously.

"Ms. Russell," he says when I enter his office. He shakes my hand firmly and waves me to a seat. "It's nice to meet you."

"You, too," I say. "Thank you for seeing me on such short notice."

"May I ask how you found me?" he says as we both sit. "If it was a referral, I'd like to thank the person in question."

"My new attorney recommended you. Alice Wills? I seem to be ass-deep in legal drama at the moment."

Mr. Chang frowns. "That doesn't sound good. I went to school with Alice. She's a good friend, and a great attorney. What can I do for you?"

"I inherited quite a bit from my father, but his entire estate went to me. My mother didn't receive anything. And I'd like to remedy that."

He takes out a legal pad and starts making notes. "Can you detail your father's estate for me?"

I shuffle through the papers in my hand and hold out the trust paperwork my father created.

"It's all here. Basically, there are three real properties, two in LA and one here in Orange County. There are 27 guitars, all valued over ten grand a piece. There's controlling interest in Plucked Strings Studios, a recording facility, also in LA. And then there's my father's music rights."

His eyes are glued to the trust. Then he raises them to me. "Joe Cruz is your father?"

I nod.

He sits back in his chair. "And what would you like your mother to have?"

"The Orange County home, for sure," I say. "Beyond that…maybe you can give me some advice. I mean, when she goes, it will all revert back to me anyway. But right now, I basically control her life, and I want her to control her own life. I don't want her to have to take care of too much, but at the same time, I want her income to be significant. So I was thinking of maybe dividing the music rights between us."

We go over all the numbers, how much income each asset brings in, how much each costs to maintain.

And then I tell him about our current legal battle.

"You need to have that resolved before we reallocate any of the assets involved," he says. "And I'd like to crunch the numbers some more and give you options. But we can give your mom her house right away."

I nod. "That's the most important piece."

"I can do that paperwork today," he says. "And the rest...how about we meet again next Thursday. We can talk over lunch at Modern Kitchen."

"You're gonna make me get dressed up, huh?"

He laughs. "I doubt the daughter of Joe Cruz has to do anything she doesn't want to do."

I shake my head. "I'm not a celebrity, Mr. Chang. And I don't wield my money that way. Being a Cruz is nothing but a burden."

His eyes soften. "Hope, I apologize. That was out of line."

"No, don't," I say. "I'm overly sensitive to it. I'm blessed, and I try not to take it for granted, but everything I have was given to me by a man I despised. He was gifted and successful, but he treated his family like dirt. I should have done this a long time ago, but I hate talking about it. I hate looking at his signature. I hate knowing I owe him."

I can't believe I just admitted all that. To a virtual stranger.

He leans forward. "My parents were Chinese immigrants. Never got a hug or a kiss from them my entire life. When I got into law school, Penn, they said, you should have gone to Harvard. When I passed the bar, they said, how many questions did you miss? When I bought my first home, they said, why doesn't it have a pool? And when I divorced my wife for being an alcoholic, they said, what did you do to drive her to drink? They owned a restaurant in China Town in LA, ran it for twenty years, but lived a very modest life. And when they passed away, to my astonishment, they left me over two million dollars in cash. I used it to start my own practice, and to put in a pool."

I smile at him. "We all have trials. I'm sorry. I didn't mean to dump on you."

"You didn't," he says. "Sometimes it's good to know we're not alone."

I nod and rise. "So Thursday. Modern Kitchen. Anything else?"

"I'll call you if there is."

He rises and shows me out.

&

After work, I throw a potato into the oven and start a chicken stir fry. Don't judge. Potatoes go with everything.

I think about Alec, about being completely successful and feeling like it's never good enough. I didn't get that, exactly, from my parents—I was just ignored. An A on a test meant nothing to them, as they were too wrapped up in their own lives—or too stoned—to care. Maybe it amounts to the same thing.

And then I think about how similar our positions are. We both profited off of our parents. The difference is, Alec used his money to be even more successful. I haven't done that. I give a healthy amount to charity, sure, and I bought my home, but I only used enough money for a down payment. I make the monthly payments with my own salary. I've never really dipped into the estate and done something significant for me.

So...if I did decide to do something, just for me...what would that be?

Chapter 6

I met Sarah through this guy Sam, the first guy I dated after my divorce. Sam and I no longer talk, but Sarah's become a good friend. We go shopping, or have lunch, and I'm teaching her to cook. And in return, Sarah has promised to get me comfortable around kids.

She's a first grade teacher. She knows a thing or two about them.

I take a personal day at work, and I meet her in her classroom before school starts. She gives me a big hug.

"Can't believe I finally got you in here," she says. "You ready for this?"

"I have to be ready?"

She laughs and goes to her desk. She hands me a large cup of coffee and a cinnamon roll. "Here. You'll need the caffeine and the sugar."

She goes over the basic structure of the day as we eat, and then the bell rings.

"Follow me," she says. "The kids line up outside, and we lead them in."

Her students are lined up in a jagged row. They're so small and cute! Sarah marches to the head of the line while I hang back.

"Everyone ready?" she says. "Daniel, we don't pick our nose. Lily, hands to yourself. Onward!"

Whoa. Sweet Sarah has morphed into a drill sergeant. Martika would love her.

She waves me to the front of the room while everyone gets settled.

"Friends, this is Ms. Russell. She's going to help us out today. While I'm taking roll, let's get your math workbooks out. You know what to do."

A little girl with red pigtails and a face full of freckles raises her hand. "Someone stole my pencil."

"What should Josephine do, friends?" Sarah asks.

"Ask her neighbor," half the class intones.

"Or?"

Several kids raise their hands. Sarah points to a girl with glasses. "Reagan?"

"She can take one from the cabinet, but her table gots to lose a point."

"That's right," Sarah says. "It's Josephine's choice."

Wow. That seems harsh. Especially if someone stole her pencil.

Josephine starts asking the other kids at her table for a loaner. I sneakily move to the cabinet in question and pull out a pencil. When I think no one's looking, I stoop next to Josephine's desk.

"Oh my gosh, look! I found your pencil!"

Josephine looks at me. "Nope. My pencil had little hearts on it."

I look at the pencil closely. "I think you're mistaken. This is definitely Josephine's pencil." I give her a wink, but the kid doesn't catch on.

"No. My pencil—"

"Was yellow," I say. And then I lower my voice and lean into her ear. "Take the pencil. Then you won't lose a point."

Understanding dawns. She takes the pencil with a smile, and I stand up. Sarah's glaring at me, but she's working to hide a smile.

I smile back.

℘

The kids are learning to borrow in subtraction. Seems like a basic concept, but the workbook has me totally lost. It's telling the kids to draw blocks—42 of them!—and visually remove 17 to see how many are left over.

Sarah looks over my shoulder. I'm helping Ethan, a cute little blonde who can't pronounce his Rs. Actually, Ethan is helping me.

"You group by tens," he tells me. "No, the extra two don't matter yet. Now take one of the tens, and subtract the seven. How much do you get?"

"Three," I say, and Ethan grins.

"Good one. So how many tens are left?"

"Three," I say, but Ethan shakes his head.

"We already subtracted the first ten. It was seventeen, not seven, remember?"

"Right," I say. "I forgot. So there are two tens left."

"Now count the ones," he says. "Three plus two is…"

"Uh…five?" I say.

"So two tens plus five is…"

I smile. "You tell me."

"I already know," he says. "You do it."

Sarah laughs, and I glare at her behind Ethan's back. "Twenty-five."

"Yes!" he cries, pumping a fist in the air. "You got it."

I swipe a hand over my brow. "Phew."

℃

The day ends with art, thank God. I thought I'd done okay in first grade, but times have changed. The whole day I've felt like an idiot.

Winter break is coming, so we're making snowflakes. Sarah demonstrates how to fold a piece of paper in fourths, and then how to cut out shapes in the paper so that when you unfold it, you get a snowflake.

This looks like fun. So I grab my own piece of paper and fold it. I pull up a small plastic blue chair next to smarty-pants Ethan, and Sarah hands me a pair of scissors.

Snowflakes are round, right? So I go around the edges of my square paper and round them all off. I notice my mistake too late, and I now have four little pieces of paper instead of one.

Ethan looks at me and laughs. "You cut the folds," he says. "Didn't you listen to Miss Klein's instructions?"

"Of course I did," I say. "I wanted four tiny snowflakes instead of one big one."

"But that's not following directions."

"This is art, isn't it?" I say back. "Isn't the artist free to create?"

Sarah goes to the front of the room. "Friends, is Ms. Russell allowed to make four tiny snowflakes instead one large one?"

"No!" the class screams. Sheesh.

"And why not? Madison?"

"'Cause she gots to follow directions."

Sarah smiles. "That's right. What should Ms. Russell do? Daniel."

"Get a new paper," he says. "And she should lose recess for not listening."

My eyes go wide. "Gee, thanks, Daniel."

The class laughs.

So I get another piece of paper.

When everyone seems to be done with this step, Sarah has the kids get the glue from their desks, and she sets out bowls of glitter among them.

"Remember, you don't need a lot of glue," she says. "Just a thin layer. The more glue you put, the longer it will take to dry." She comes over to me. "Let's go around and help them with the glue. And after they sprinkle glitter, help them tip the excess back into the bowls."

I wander around. Some kids are meticulous, putting dots of glue and little pinches of glitter on top. Some squeeze the bottles for all they're worth and use their fingers to smear the glue. Daniel has managed to squeeze out half his bottle, and glue covers both of his hands and the tip of snotty nose.

"Need some help with that?" I ask.

He shakes his head. "I got it."

Then he takes the bowl and dumps the entire thing on his snowflake.

"Whoa, there," I say. I take the bowl from him and set it down. "Why don't you wash your hands, and I'll get the glitter?"

He goes to the sink, and I try to gingerly pick up his creation without messing it up. But the glue has made it all soggy and floppy. I finally get it flat in my hands and move it over the bowl.

"You done yet?" Daniel asks. I look down at him, and he's still covered in glue.

"Not yet. Almost."

I start to tip the snowflake in, and without warning, another kid grabs the bowl. The glitter slides off onto the top of the desk. I sigh. And then I feel a tap on my leg.

"You done yet?" Daniel asks again. "Hey. You done?" He puts both hands on my legs.

And I take a step back to get away from his gluey hands, but I back into little Liam's chair, and I trip. It's like slow motion. I feel myself fall. I try to keep Daniel's snowflake safe, but the edge of it sticks to my hair and is ripped from my hands, I tumble backwards right onto poor Liam, and I reach a hand out to catch myself, and my hand ends up smack dab on Liam's snowflake.

And I keep on tumbling backwards.

My head hits the corner of a desk at the next table over and I'm out.

Chapter 7

An EMT leans over me and pulls my eyelids up.

"Can you speak?" he asks.

I lick my lips. "Yeah. I'm okay."

"Don't try to sit up," he says. He cradles my head and examines the back, parting my hair along the scalp. "This is pretty deep. You need stitches."

"Stitches?" I whisper. "I'm bleeding?"

He takes some gauze out of his medical kit and holds it to my head. "Who's the teacher here?"

I can't see Sarah, but I can hear her voice behind me. "I am."

"Let's get the kids outside," he says. "They don't need to see this."

Sarah gathers the kids, and I hear the door open. The EMT starts cleaning my cut.

"Do you feel dizzy?"

"A bit."

"Do you feel nauseated?"

I grimace. "If I think about the stitches."

He laughs. "Like I said, don't move. I've stabilized your neck. It's just a precaution."

I gulp. "You think I broke my neck?"

"I don't know," he says honestly. "The 911 call said you were unconscious. That was over seven minutes ago, and you weren't awake until I roused you."

I can't process this. Seven minutes…I don't remember being unconscious at all.

And I have a neck brace on? Oh my God, I've lost seven minutes of my life!

A sneaky tear leaks from my eye. "I've had five concussions," I say. "Is that important for you to know?"

He stops working on my head and looks at me. "Five? Were any recent?"

"No."

"How?"

My throat is tight. "Rough childhood."

His eyes soften. "We'll take care of you. The guys are bringing a stretcher in. Just hang in there. And if you feel like you need to vomit, let me know."

∽

Sarah is holding my hand in a little emergency room cubicle when my mother bursts in.

"Hope!" she yells. She throws her body over mine and hugs tight.

I pat her back. "I'm fine, Ma. Everything's fine."

"Fine? You're in a hospital! What happened?"

"I fell and hit my head. School is a dangerous place."

"School?" she cries. "What were you doing in school?"

I sigh. "You haven't met Sarah. Sarah, this is my mom, Rosalyn. Sarah's a first grade teacher. I was helping out."

Sarah gives my mother a tentative smile.

"Do you have a concussion?"

"Yes," I say, "but it's mild. No bleeding in the brain. Just a few stitches."

"How many?"

"Thirty-two."

"Thirty-two," she whispers. "Where?"

I point to my head, and my mother leans in for a look.

"They shaved half your hair off!"

I look at the ceiling. "It was that, or bleed all over myself. Stop it, okay? I'm fine."

She takes out her phone. "Can you sit up a bit?"

"You are not taking pictures."

"This will make a fabulous Snapchat story," she says. "People love this shit."

Sarah looks at me. I roll my eyes.

"Sarah, dear," my mother says as she snaps a final photo, "could you go to Hope's house and pack her a bag?"

"Of course," Sarah says, but I jump in.

"I'm not staying with you, Ma. I only need a babysitter for one night. Why don't you come stay at my house?"

"You have all those guitars in your spare bedroom," she says. "They creep me out."

I sigh. "Sarah, you don't have to."

"It's the least I can do," she says. "I almost killed you."

"Thanks," I say with a smile. "I have a travel bag that's already stocked, in the bathroom cabinet. Just some sweats and underwear would be great." She fishes my keys out of my purse. My mother gives Sarah her address, Sarah plants a smack on my forehead, and she leaves.

"How soon can you get out of here?" my mother asks, pulling up a chair.

"They're getting the release paperwork done now. Shouldn't be too long. What time is it?"

"Close to midnight. My phone died, or I would have gotten your message sooner. Are you in pain?" She takes my hand and squeezes tight, and then she looks down. "What is all over your hands?"

"Glue," I say. "And glitter."

"It's in your hair, too. Why?"

I just sigh.

Chapter 8

I get through the night with my mother and settle back at home. Day two of a concussion…sucks. I've been through this enough to know. My head feels like one of those punchball balloons, while it's being punched.

But I refuse to take pain meds. Nope. No drugs for me.

I prop my laptop on my knees and check my email. Huh. Someone from the *Cupid's Lair* website messaged me. I click on the link, and it takes me to my dashboard on the site. The message is from Nick Martelli, the divorced father of three I contacted with Martika.

Hope, thanks for getting in touch. I admit, I haven't had much luck on this site, and I'm thinking my profile is to blame—I have more baggage than Samsonite (ha,ha). Reading your profile struck a chord with me. I think you went the honesty route, too, and that's important to me. Not to get too heavy too early, but I'm not playing around. I want to find a serious relationship, and it sounds like you're looking for that, too.

I have a few deal breakers, so I might as well get them out there. No drugs, no heavy drinking, no felonies. I have three kids, ages 10, 13, and 16, and while I won't involve them with my "dates" until I develop a commitment, I want a partner who will be a good role model. I share custody and have them with me every other week. They are my highest priority.

Boy, I've got you running for the hills, don't I? Seriously, though, I'm a pretty good guy. I run my own software company, I play golf and tennis, and I love going to concerts and movies. I also love to travel, but I haven't done much traveling since my divorce (three years ago). I need a traveling buddy.

Tell me about yourself and what you're looking for. I'm looking forward to getting to know you better.

Nick

Huh.

Brutal honesty is good, if a little awkward. But that's what dating is—awkward.

I kind of like this whole setup. I can get to know a guy without any pressure. No uncomfortable eye contact, no wondering if he's going to kiss me, no worries about my makeup or my breath. Maybe Martika knew what she was doing.

Nick, thanks for the reply. I love that you have a sense of humor about things while still taking this whole thing seriously.

No drugs, I only drink socially and quit when I get sleepy (which is way before I get drunk), no run-ins with the law. Sounds like we're good there.

I admit, I was hesitant to contact you because of the age difference, but I feel like a bit of an old soul. I was with my childhood sweetheart for 17 years (10 married), and we divorced a year ago. No kids. Three teens are a bit intimidating, but I'm open to it. As an only child, I've always wanted a large family.

I play tennis, never tried golf, love concerts and travel. Since my divorce, I've been getting adventurous and have been trying new hobbies. I play several instruments, and my music is important to me. This past year has been a process of discovery. I didn't realize how little I knew myself as an individual, a person outside of my marriage.

My idea of a great relationship would be one where we can both be individuals, but being a couple makes us stronger. Where we communicate openly and often, give and receive support, and where we are each other's greatest champions.

Does the age difference give you pause? What are you looking for?

Hope

I agonize over the message for an hour, then I finally hit send.

My phone rings, a number I don't recognize.

"Hello?"

"Uh, hi. Is this Glitter Girl?" a deep voice asks.

"Glitter Girl?" I ask. "I think you have the wrong number."

He laughs. "Is this Hope?"

I hesitate. "Yes."

"My name is Noah. I'm the EMT that treated you when you hit your head yesterday. I wanted to see if you're okay."

"You had those gorgeous eyelashes," I blurt out without thinking. "I'd kill for lashes like yours."

Noah laughs again. "Eyelashes...okay, I'll take it. At least you remember me."

I laugh, too. "Sorry. I have a raging headache and no ability to filter right now. But I appreciate the follow-up call. This is a first."

"This isn't exactly a professional call," he says. "And if you're in pain, I should let you go. Rest. Maybe I can call you in a few days."

"For what?" I ask.

"Well...I was talking with your friend, Sarah. The teacher? She gave me your number."

I blink through the pain and try to figure this out. "And?"

"And...I thought maybe if you want, I can take you out some time."

"Oh." I was about to tell him about my pain level, the slight nausea, the throbbing behind my left ear.

But that's not why he called.

"Uh...it's Noah, right?"

"Yes. Good memory. Especially for someone with a head injury."

I laugh. "I'm open to that. Except, yeah, I need a few days. Maybe you can text me next week?"

"I'll do that," he says, and there's an erotic promise in his voice. It makes me shiver. "I'm sorry I called so soon. Patience isn't my strong suit. So get back to healing, and we'll talk soon."

"Okay," I say. "And thanks for calling."

"Later, Glitter Girl."

I laugh. "Later, Noah."

I just stare at my phone. How weird was that?

And the phone rings again, startling me. It's my attorney, Alec Chang.

Butterflies unexpectedly tumble in my stomach.

"Mr. Chang," I say. "How are you?"

"I'm well, Hope. And please, call me Alec. I'm just following up on the paperwork I had messengered to you. Did everything look alright?"

"I haven't looked at it yet," I admit. "Actually, I had an accident yesterday. Thirty-two stitches in my head and seven hours in the ER. I probably won't get to it until tomorrow."

"Are you alright?" he asks, concern in his voice. "What happened?"

"I'm fine," I say. "I tripped and hit my head. Stupid, really. But I can't take pain meds, so it'll be a slow recovery."

"Is there anything I can do?" he asks. "I can have my assistant run some errands if you need it."

I smile. "I really appreciate that, but I'm fine. I don't know if I can make Thursday, though. Let me see how I feel."

"You recover and don't worry about the meeting. I'll follow up and see how you're doing. Just get better soon."

"Thanks, Alec. Take care."

"You, too, Hope. I mean that. Take care of yourself."

Double huh.

There was something in Alec's voice, a genuine concern for me. Hmmm. Gonna chalk it up to great customer service for the legacy of the Cruz dynasty.

All this communication has me exhausted. I snuggle into my pillow and sleep.

Chapter 9

Martika rouses me just after six. She gets a fresh bag of ice for me and lays it on the top of my head.

"Lift your feet," she says, and as I do, she sits down where my feet were and settles them on her lap. She rubs my toes, and I sigh in contentment.

"Thanks," I say. "This is the first time I've really been sick since the divorce. I didn't realize how awful it is to be alone and in pain."

"Nurse Martika to the rescue," she says. "It's a good thing I'm over the morning sickness. Can you imagine the two of us, rocking back and forth on the couch, moaning in unison?"

I smile. "Matt and I both had food poisoning once. It was awful. We were in that one-bedroom apartment, one bathroom, and I was hurling in the sink while he was shitting his brains out. Then we'd switch. Ugh."

"Ah, marriage," she says. "How's the legal crap coming?"

"Fine," I say. "Guess what? That divorced guy Nick responded back to me on *Cupid's Lair*."

Martika smiles. "And?"

"And then the EMT that came to my rescue called me and asked me on a date."

She laughs. "That's awesome. Was he good-looking?"

"Very. And then…I kind of have a small little thing for my estate lawyer."

She raises an eyebrow. "Don't tell me he asked you out, too."

I smile. "No. But there's something there. He was very concerned when I told him about my accident."

She shakes her head. "Three men. Wow. Are you gonna date them all at once?"

"Of course not," I say. "I mean, only one officially asked me out. It's just kind of nice to have options."

"I don't know," she says. "Too many options in love is not a good thing. You're gonna start comparing them, feeling guilty if you kiss one and not the other…"

I laugh. "I haven't even gone on a date with any of them. I can't count my chickens before they hatch."

"They're cocks, not chickens," she says.

We both laugh.

The doorbell rings. Martika answers it and comes back to the couch carrying a huge bouquet of wildflowers and a gift basket.

"Man number three has struck," she says. "They're from Alec Chang & Associates."

She sets them on the coffee table, and I pull out the card.

Hope, here's to a speedy recovery. Let me know if there's anything I can do. Alec

"How sweet," I say. I dive into the basket. There are apples, Band-Aids, chocolate, a bottle of wine (*Better than pain meds!* a handwritten note attached to the neck says), a heatable neck wrap, an eye mask, fluffy socks, and a box of fortune cookies.

"Holy crap," Martika says. "I want stitches. What's with the fortune cookies?"

"His parents owned a Chinese restaurant," I say. "It's a nod to the story he told me."

"I thought he bought this basket off the Internet," she says. "You mean, he put it together himself?"

"Looks like it," I say. I show her the note on the wine bottle. "I told him I can't take pain meds."

She smiles. "I think you're right. There's something there."

&

Martika tucks me in bed. I've got my fluffy socks on and the microwaved wrap around my neck. She leaves, and I know I need to sleep, but this headache is making sleep impossible.

So I go back to *Cupid's Lair*. Nick has sent me a new message.

Dear Hope,

It's weird, isn't it, getting out of a long relationship? When I first moved out, I was at a loss. I had an entire apartment to decorate all by myself, and I had no idea what I was doing. I basically set up one bookcase to look exactly like a bookcase we'd had in our living room, and then I thought, what am I doing? I don't HAVE to put pictures of Vanessa on this shelf, and pictures of Caleb on another. I can do anything I want! So I mixed all the pictures up. Silly, I know, but it was a freeing moment for me. So I know how you feel.

What am I looking for? My ideal partner would be someone I have shared interests with, and someone who is content if I have to work late on a Friday night. Because I own my own biz, yes, I work a lot. But I also have more freedom, too. I can meet you for lunch, or take off work to watch my son play soccer, but you might have to have dinner with friends and meet me after for drinks. I'm pretty good at balancing (now, I wasn't always this good), and I keep my commitments. I guess I'm saying that I'd like a partner who understands all that.

As far as the physical…if your profile picture is accurate, all I can say is WOW. No worries there. I'm not necessarily looking for someone under thirty, but I'm open. As I said, I haven't had a lot of luck, but it's not because I've been overly picky, I don't think. A lot of the women I've met are looking for someone to take care of them. I want to take care of my partner in an equal way, but if…sigh. I'm not a sugar daddy, and that's what my profile projects, apparently. Let's leave it at that.

Tell me about your perfect date.

Nick

So I open a new message and type.

Nick, I had a moment similar to yours with the bookcase, but for me, it was my fridge. I was used to having Tabasco sauce and IPA beer stocked at all times. I bought those things after the divorce, only out of habit, and when I finally figured out how nice it would be to have a Corona in my fridge…there wasn't any room. I dumped all the IPAs down the sink, and suddenly my fridge was half empty. I think that sums up divorce nicely. :)

My perfect partner helps. If I'm cooking dinner, which I love to do, I'd love it if he came into the kitchen and kept me company rather than watching TV. If I come home from the store and have a ton of bags, if my partner is there and not busy, I'd like him to help bring the bags in. He'd have to be okay with me playing guitar. He'd give me time to spend with friends and not make me feel guilty about it.

Physical appearance is not particularly important to me, but I liked your picture right away. So no worries. :)

My perfect date is spent at home, actually. Just the two of us, music, cooking a meal, sharing stories, being silly, being intimate. I enjoy going out, but since you asked for my perfect date…there it is.

I'd love to meet for coffee. Let me know what your perfect date is and if you're interested.

Hope

I yawn. I almost shut my laptop, but I suddenly see three dots pop up under my message. Nick is typing right now!

So I wait…

Can you do coffee in the morning before work? I don't even know if you have a 9-5 job, but there's a great place halfway between us—The Grinder on 10th St? I have a 9:00, but if we meet at 7, that gives us two hours. The rest of my day is booked, and I'd rather not wait two days to meet you. Nick

Whoa. A seven AM date…that's a new one. I can push through the pain, but my hair…fuck it. If he's gonna test me with an early-morning date, I can test him with a shaved head.

Yes, I have a 9-5, but I have this week off. I'll see you there at 7. Good night, Nick.

Chapter 10

The pain this morning has backed off a bit, but my stitches have started to itch. Nick will probably think I have lice, the way I keep scratching at it.

It's December and freezing, so I don't have a lot of choice as far as wardrobe goes. Jeans, tight sweater, knee-high stiletto boots. My purple wool swing coat. Hair in a ponytail to hide that half of it's gone.

It's five after seven when I pull into the parking lot. There's already a line, and I notice Nick right away, near the front. He's in a black suit, polished back shoes, shiny cobalt blue tie. Mmm. He looks good.

Recognition hits him as the door swings closed behind me. He smiles wide, and I make my way over to him.

"So glad you could make it," he says, giving me a kiss on the cheek. "I was worried I'd scare you off with the early date."

"Not remotely," I say with a smile. "I love a man who's up and around early."

He grins. "Then you're gonna love me."

The line moves forward, and it's our turn. "What's your pleasure?" he asks me.

"Tall coffee black," I say. "No room for cream."

"Same," he says to the girl. "Anything to eat?"

"No, thank you."

We get our coffees and get settled at a table.

"Are you sure you're not hungry?" he says.

I tell him about my accident, and that my stomach's off. He winces in sympathy.

"I can't believe you came to meet me this morning," he says. "You should be in bed."

"I'd rather be here." Nick smiles, and his teeth are straight and white. "Tell me about your kids."

He ducks his head. "Caleb is 13, into soccer and basketball. Lucy is 10, a girly-girl, very social and bubbly and always wanting to be in the spotlight. And Vanessa is 16 going on 26. Bright, sweet…but she takes too much on herself. Especially since the divorce. I'd love to be able to get her to loosen up."

I smile. "She sounds like me. My parents divorced when I was 14, and I think I took everything too seriously. Maybe still do."

"I'm trying not to put too much responsibility on her," he says, "but she takes it anyway. I wish she had more fun."

"Is it necessary for her to be more responsible?" I ask. "I mean, is your ex-wife pulling her weight?"

He laughs. "Maybe not in the way I'd like, but yes."

"Then I think you have to let your daughter do what she needs to do. I mean, give her opportunities to be a kid, but don't make her feel bad for taking things seriously. It's a good problem to have. I think most parents of teens are trying to get their kids to be more responsible, not less."

He smiles. "True. They're great kids. I really have nothing to complain about. What about you?"

"You mean kids?" I ask, and he nods. "I don't have any, but I would like to have a few. Are you open to having more?"

"With the right woman." He holds my gaze.

"Is that a line, or are you serious?"

Nick laughs. "I'm serious. But it would have to happen soon. I don't think I want babies after 50."

I smile. "Fair enough."

"So tell me about your job."

I fiddle with the rim of my coffee cup. "I'm a technical writer. Beyond that, I'm financially independent. No sugar daddy needed."

He smiles. "Did you win the lottery?"

I shake my head. "My dad passed away and left me his estate."

"What did he do?"

"Music," I say.

"Would I know him?"

I nod.

Nick reaches across the table and takes my hand. "Don't tell me yet. Let's get to know each other without the other stuff."

Huh. "Okay. What about the rest of your family? Are your parents around?"

He nods. "They live two streets over from me. I grew up in Newport. Two brothers live in Orange County, too, and we're close. They're younger than me, and their kids are younger, but we still get along."

I sigh and prop my chin in my hand. "I love that. You are very lucky. I'm an only child, and the little extended family I do have…we don't talk."

"I'm sorry," he says. "That must be hard."

I shrug. "It's not all bad. I have my mom, and we're close. Although…"

"What?"

I cringe. "She's only seven years older than you."

Nick laughs. "How do you think she'd feel about that?"

"Honestly…I'm not sure. I never can tell with her."

"Does she live nearby?" he asks.

I nod. "Same city, five minutes apart. But she'll be supportive, I think. She just wants me to be happy."

We chat for another hour nonstop. Nick is interesting and funny and intelligent. He's a bit on the stuffy side, but I don't mind that.

Suddenly his phone beeps. He takes it out and pushes a few buttons. "That's my alarm. I have five minutes before I need to leave."

"You set an alarm?" I ask.

"I didn't want to be rude and constantly check my phone. This way I know how much time I have to ask you out again."

I smile. "You want to ask me out?"

He nods. "Are you busy tomorrow night?"

I pretend to think about it. "I think tomorrow night works."

"Are you comfortable with me picking you up? Or would you rather meet me somewhere?"

"You can pick me up," I say. "I've never had that. A real date."

I told Nick my dating history, but he still seems surprised. "Okay, then. How's six?"

I give him my address, and he walks me to my car.

I pause, fiddling with my keys.

"Thanks for the coffee," I say. "I had a good time."

"Me, too." He gives me a warm hug, and then a kiss on the cheek. But I don't let him go.

He pulls back, just enough to look in my eyes, and my brain goes fuzzy. His eyes are a copper hazel, with flecks of orange. He blinks.

"Hope," he whispers, and I push up on my toes and our lips meet.

The kiss is tender, soft. And then I open my eyes and find him staring at me, and I deepen the kiss. Nick responds. I drop my keys and put my arms around him, and I feel his hands flatten against my back and squeeze.

"That was unexpected," he whispers against my lips.

I pull back an inch. "Too much?"

"God, no," he says, kissing me again, and suddenly we're sucking face like two teenagers. We both break out in a laugh, and Nick hugs me to his chest.

"I'm looking forward to tomorrow night," I say.

Nick grins. "Me, too."

Chapter 11

I get home close to ten, and there's Matt, in blazer and jeans—his teaching clothes—waiting for me on the front steps. He jumps to his feet and rushes to my door as I pull in the driveway.

"What are you doing?" he says. "You shouldn't be driving!"

"Who told you?" I ask, shrugging him off as he tries to take my arm and help me out of the car.

"Benny. Why didn't you call me?"

I sigh. "Matt, I appreciate the concern, but I'm fine. Why would I call you?"

He follows me to the front door. "You've had five concussions that we know about, and probably lots more that we don't. You need to take care of yourself."

I open the door, and Matt follows me in.

"I'm fine," I repeat. "What are you doing here?"

He glances around, like he's not quite sure himself. "Benny said you were unconscious for ten minutes." As if that explains his presence.

"Seven."

"Seven minutes, Hope! Jesus! Get out of those boots and lie down. I'll rub your head."

Tears sting my eyes. "We're divorced," I say, my voice all croaky. "You divorced me! Why are you doing this?"

"You were hurt, and I wasn't there!" he screams. "Do you know how much that kills me?"

I swallow hard. "I'm sorry you feel guilty, but this is on you. This was your decision. You're not my husband anymore. You don't get to ride in and save me."

He stares at me helplessly.

"And frankly, I don't need your sword and shield anymore. I'm doing okay on my own."

"Don't say that," he says. "We both know you've never done well on your own."

I fold my arms over my chest. "Thanks. Thanks for reminding me that I'm grateful you left."

"Shit, I didn't mean it like that."

"That's exactly how you meant it," I say. "And you're right. I relied on you, and you let me down, and I had to figure out how to stand on my own two feet. You're not upset that I got hurt. You're upset that I don't need you anymore."

He clenches his hands into fists. "That's not true. I know I left, but I still care about you."

A tear slides down my cheek. "You don't have that right. I mean, you do, but you'll have to care about me from afar. I can't do this, Matt."

"Do what?"

"This! I'm moving on. I'm trying to get on with my life. But I can't do that if you keep showing up!"

He fights to hide a smile. "So you still care about me, too."

I throw my hands up. "Of course I do! I always will. But now we've dated other people, slept with other people…we can't go back."

His eyes narrow. "You've slept with other people?"

"Don't you dare," I say. "You cheated on me with a fucking grad student. At least I waited until the ink was dry on our divorce papers."

He looks away.

"You've been acting really strange," I say, "and I know communication has never been your strong suit, but why don't you just come clean. What do you want from me?"

He sighs. "Jesus, Hope."

"If I can yell at you, and I can stand here and listen to you yell at me, you can certainly be honest."

He stamps his foot, like a two-year-old having a temper tantrum. "I don't know what I want, okay? I just know that…"

I wait patiently.

"I miss you."

"Is it me you miss, or do you miss my cooking? My laundry skills? My amazing back rubs?"

He smiles. "And your music. The house is fucking empty without it."

I force myself not to smile back. "Are you dating anyone now?"

"No," he says.

"I am. And I'm not gonna screw it up for someone who doesn't know what he wants."

He shoves his hands into his front pockets. "And what if I figure it out? What I want?"

I shrug. "We don't always get what we want."

Chapter 12

I open the door to software-mogul Nick in jeans and a navy v-neck sweater. He gives me a single red rose and a tight hug.

"You look beautiful," he says.

I blush. "Thanks. Let me put this in some water, and we can go."

"Nice home," he says as he follows me to the kitchen. "Did you pick the colors?"

I laugh. Every wall is a different color, and yes, I picked them all. "I did. I like bright."

"I noticed that with the purple coat."

I find a vase and fill it with water. "What's your house like?"

"White," he says. "I don't have much patience for decorating. But this is…interesting. It's homey and artistic at the same time."

"My ex wouldn't let me paint our house," I say. "Not the way I wanted to. He was worried about resale value."

Nick smiles. "I'm guessing you're not worried."

I give a mock pout. "Are you saying that no one would like this house the way I decorated it?"

He holds up his hands. "Not at all. I meant that you must feel settled. Like you won't be moving any time soon."

Rose watered, I pick up my purse. "That's true. I love this house."

He takes my hand and leads me to his car, a Maserati. He holds the door open for me and helps me in.

"So where are we going?" I ask as we drive.

"You'll see."

We chat on the drive, and fifteen minutes later, we pull up to the beach in Laguna. Nick pulls out three blankets and a basket from his trunk, and we walk down to the sand. He lays out one of the blankets, and we both sit.

He rummages in the basket and pulls out two Coronas and a bottle opener. He flips the tops and hands me one.

"You remembered the Corona?" I ask.

He smiles. "I hope you were serious with that story. And yesterday you told me about your love of Italian food, so I brought spaghetti."

I smile. "That was thoughtful. Thank you."

We eat and we drink. Nick tucks a blanket around me as the chilly December wind picks up. I have a nice two-beer buzz going when he pulls me down beside him and points to the sky.

"Do you know the constellations?" he asks.

"Most of them," I say. "I took astronomy in college, thinking it would be about the moon and the stars. Turned into a math nightmare, but some of it stuck. There's Orion and his belt…the Pleiades…the Big Dipper."

He turns on his side toward me. "You constantly surprise me."

I flip to my side and face him. "Don't know why. You don't know me yet."

Nick smiles. "I know. I guess I just had this preconceived notion about 28-year-olds. And you don't fit any of them."

"Is that supposed to be a compliment?" I ask.

He laughs. "Tell me you don't have a few preconceived notions about a 45-year-old father."

I smile. "You're right. I have wondered."

"About what?"

"Sex," I whisper. "What does your body look like, feel like? Will you be teaching me things, or will you struggle to keep up?"

Nick laughs again. "Fuck. That's not what I expected you to say."

"Well?"

"If there's something you want to know," he says, "ask."

"Okay. How's your stamina?"

He wriggles a little closer to me. "I run five miles every morning. Never had a complaint."

I grin. "Is the hair on the rest of your body going gray, too?"

He smiles. "You'll have to figure that one out yourself."

"And how long does a 45-year-old man usually date his...dates, before he sleeps with them?"

"A 45-year-old man knows how to read his date," he says. "He waits for the proper time. Could be one date, could be ten."

"So he's not waiting for marriage," I say.

Nick's eyes go wide. "Are you?"

"No."

He laughs. "What do 28-year-old women want? How do they decide that the time is right?"

I prop myself on one elbow and look down at him. "I don't have a lot of data to go on. But I want to wait until I'm completely comfortable. I want the sex to be amazing."

Nick props himself up, too. "What do you need to be comfortable?"

"I need to feel like I can share anything, even the bad stuff, and still be accepted."

His eyes soften. "What kind of bad stuff?"

I shake my head. "I don't want to ruin this moment. I'm sure you haven't had a perfect life, either."

"I was a pothead in high school," he says, and I laugh. "I was lucky I graduated."

"I appreciate the honesty," I say, "but that's not what I meant."

Nick slips his hand in mine and squeezes. "You can tell me, Hope. I won't think less of you or judge."

His eyes are so sincere. His voice…so soft. But I don't want to be pitied. There's plenty of time for that.

"Soon," I say. "It's just about how I grew up, not about anything particularly bad I did myself. Someday I'll share."

He nods. "So what are you doing tomorrow besides playing hooky?"

I smile. "Actually, I'm meeting my mom for lunch. I have a surprise for her."

Nick raises an eyebrow.

"I'm finally signing over the deed to her house to her. It was my dad's house, but they lived there their entire marriage, and it should have been hers all along, but she signed an iron-clad prenup. I should have done it a long time ago."

"Have you consulted an attorney?" he asks. "There could be tax implications."

I frown. "Yes, *Dad*, I have an attorney."

Nick groans, and I flop backwards.

"I shouldn't have said that," I say. "Sorry."

"No," he says, "I overstepped. I apologize."

"No, you didn't," I say. "You were just giving advice. I should be able to take advice." I sit up and look out at the waves.

Nick sits up, too. "This is a problem, isn't it?"

I turn and look at him. "Maybe. But only if you see me as young and incompetent, and only if I see you as wise and all-knowing. And you have to accept that I will make mistakes, and I have to accept that you have life experience to share."

He shoves a hand through his hair. "I can't deny that I feel a little bit…wiser."

"And I feel a little bit young. But I can fight it if you can."

Nick takes my hand. "I'm willing to try."

I lean forward. "Did you feel that I was young and incompetent when I kissed you?"

He drops my hand and places his hands on my cheeks. "Do it again," he whispers.

Our mouths meet, and his tongue slips between my lips. His hands slide into my hair, and I crush my chest to his, and then the tips of his fingers dig into my wound. I wince and gasp, pulling back.

"Oh, shit, did I hurt you?" He grabs my arm tenderly, concern crinkling at the corners of his eyes.

I breathe through the pain. "It's okay. No harm done."

"That's a lie," he says. He gets to his feet and pulls me up beside him. "Let's get you home."

He packs up and drives me home, walking me to my door and even taking my keys and unlocking the house for me.

"Thank you, Nick," I say at the door. "Thank you for such a thoughtful date."

"I'd really like to see you again," he says. "Maybe this weekend?"

My head is pounding. "I'd like that. Call me tomorrow."

He gives me a sweet kiss and a wave, and I shut the door.

Christ.

I go to the bathroom, and my stomach churns. I flip on the light and try to look at my wound, but it's in exactly the wrong place. I touch a finger to it, and it comes away tacky with blood. So I get a clean cloth and hold it on my head. I kick off my shoes and curl up in bed. As soon as the pain lessens, I'll get out of these sandy jeans.

Instead, I fall asleep.

80

I wake to the doorbell. That had never happened to me in my life, until a month ago when Matt's parents' house was on fire, and he needed a late-night babysitter for his dog. And now. That's twice. What's with the midnight emergencies?

But as I swing my legs off the side of the bed, I realize it's light out, completely light out. My clock says 9:30. Crap.

I push to my feet, and the room spins. Whoa. I grab the edge of my dresser for support. Guess I got up too fast. So I keep a hand on the furniture, and the wall, and gingerly walk to the door.

The doorbell rings again.

"Who is it?" I yell when I finally have the door in sight.

"Alec Chang," a voice calls.

"I'm coming." But to get to the door, I have to cross the open space to the foyer, without any support. My vision blurs.

"Hope?"

"Coming," I say again, but I know my voice is barely louder than a whisper. I have to get to the door.

Suddenly the knob is in my hands. I don't remember walking this far. I twist it, but the door won't open.

"Hope?"

"I can't…Alec, I can't…"

"Open the door, Hope. Can you open the door?"

Apparently I can. Because I'm suddenly staring at Alec from inches away, and he's holding me up.

"It's okay," he says as I slide to the floor. "Hold on. I've got you…"

Chapter 13

I wake up two days later and a pint of blood lighter. Well, I was a pint of blood lighter, until they gave me that transfusion.

Apparently I tore open some of the stitches, the deep ones, and I bled all night long. I was lucky that Alec arrived when he did.

And though, as a rule, I don't take pain meds...the nurses give it to me without asking. I sleep better than I've slept in weeks.

My mother insists on keeping me at her house. After going it alone the first go-round, I'm grateful. Even if the house stinks of Tahitian vanilla and her weird Patchouli incense.

It's been three days since I got out of the hospital, and my mother's barely let me pee by myself. I feel pretty good this morning, so I get up, place a plastic shower cap over my head, and take a shower.

God, does the hot water feel good.

I get back to my room and throw my towel on the bed. My mother actually put my clothes away in her dresser drawers, as though I'd moved in. I open the top drawer. Weird, this is so weird. Feels like I'm back in high school. Now, where did she put my underwear?

I close the drawer, bend down, and open the bottom one. Bingo.

And the bedroom door creaks open.

"She'll be so glad to see you," my mother says, and then she gasps.

I turn at the intrusion, my Captain America thong dangling from my fingers, and there is my mother and Alec.

I duck down behind the bed. "Ma!"

"Sorry, sorry," she says, a laugh in her voice. "I thought you were in bed."

"You thought wrong!" I yell.

"I'll just make us some tea," she says, closing the door.

Shit. I slide to my butt and stifle a giggle. Alec Chang just got a great view of both my ass and my boobs.

And me, in a shower cap.

So much for my little crush.

∞

Okay, so I dally. I dilly. I try to put off the inevitable, but my mother finally yells at me.

"Hope, come on, how long does it take to get dressed?"

So I steel my spine and exit the room.

"Hey, Alec," I say. "Ma, can you give us a minute?"

She huffs, but she stands and goes to her room.

Alec stands, too. "Hope, I am so sorry. I didn't see anything, I swear."

"Liar."

"You can't prove otherwise," he says. "But, damn."

I laugh. "Guess there's not much I can do about it. I could ask you to strip. A little tit for tat."

His mouth quirks up in a grin. "You have to buy me dinner first."

"The gentleman always pays."

"Tonight," he says. "Let me make you dinner." He takes my arm and guides me to the couch. "I'm serious."

"Isn't that against the ethics code? Dating a client?" I ask.

"I quit," he says. "I can pass your stuff to one of my associates."

I shake my head. "Why?"

"Honestly? I don't know. I haven't stopped thinking about you since we met. You told that story about your dad, and I just…I felt something. I haven't felt something in a long time."

"I felt it too," I say. "I told my best friend that there was something there."

"Are you going back home today?"

I nod. "Although I'm not looking forward to the cleanup."

"It's done," he says. "I got a cleaning crew in there."

"Thank you," I say, my eyes stinging a bit. "It's been weighing on me. I can't believe you thought of that."

"I saw the carnage," he says. "You bled all over the floor. I thought you'd been stabbed."

"Shit."

We smile at one another.

"So I can come over tonight and cook for you?" he asks.

"You cook, huh?"

"Family biz."

I smile. "Then it's a date."

My mother comes out with my phone pressed to her ear.

"You can't fire her! She's been in the hospital! Of course we have a doctor's note! Fine. You'll be hearing from my attorney!"

I stand. "They fired me?"

She waves a hand. "It won't stick. What an asshole your boss is." And then my phone rings, and she answers it without asking me. "Who is this? Nick? Nick who? This is Hope's mother. She's been in the hospital. Yes, she tore some stitches and almost bled to death. Why didn't she call you? She was at death's door! Why don't you call her in a few days?"

I wince.

"Who's Nick?" she demands.

"A friend," I say. "Although I don't know if he'll want to be my friend anymore after that."

She tosses my phone at me. "You need new friends."

I look at Alec. She's right.

Chapter 14

Alec shows up on time for dinner, but instead of groceries, he's carrying take-out bags.

"I hope you don't mind," he says. "My last appointment ran late, and I'm out of energy. Rain check on the homemade meal?"

I take a bag from him. "No problem. What are we eating?"

"The best macaroni and cheese in the world," he says.

I raise an eyebrow. "No way. From Haven Gastropub?"

"You know it?"

I grin. "Know it? It's my favorite restaurant!"

Alec shakes his head as we move to the kitchen and open the bags. "I can't believe that. I eat there at least twice a week. It's a five-minute walk from my house."

I grab us each a beer. "You live in Old Towne Orange? I love that area."

"Me, too," he says as we sit and dig in. "I've always loved the architecture, particularly the Arts and Crafts style. Before my divorce, we lived in Irvine, land of the tract home. I wanted a house with some character."

"I almost bought there after my divorce," I say, "but I decided to stay close to my mom."

"So family's important to you?"

I nod. "As you know, I didn't have a great family growing up. But my ex's family was pretty solid. I know we can't all be born to the perfect family, but I want my kids to be."

"I have a huge family," he says. "My dad was the only boy of eight kids, and my aunts all relied on him and looked up to him. And now they're intent on taking care of me."

"Are they all local?"

Alec nods. "LA, but the two-hour drive doesn't deter them. If I never wanted to do another load of laundry or take another trip to the grocery store, I'd be set."

I laugh. "I can't imagine that." And then my eyes sting and I blink.

"What's wrong?"

I shake my head. "It's silly."

"I don't mind silly."

I force myself to smile. "I just realized…I've never had that. Family I could totally rely on no matter what. I mean, I have my best friend, and she's amazing, and my mom's okay now, but…ugh. Ignore me. I'm fine."

"It's okay to share what you're feeling," he says.

"But I sound pitiful."

"You sound like you've been through some tough things, and you're trying to find your way out. There's nothing wrong with that."

"Thanks," I say, giving him a genuine smile.

Alec smiles back. "So do you play guitar like your dad?"

"I wouldn't say I play like my dad, but I play."

"My parents forced clarinet lessons on me. Seven years. You can imagine my dating life in high school."

"High school girls are stupid. I can appreciate a clarinet player."

Alec shudders. "I still have nightmares about it."

I laugh. "I have a clarinet. Will you play something?"

He gapes at me. "You own a clarinet? Do you know how to play it?"

"Not really," I say. "A little bit. I like the way it sounds."

He shakes his head. "Too bad we didn't meet when I was sixteen. You would have been all over me."

⁓

We spend five hours lingering over dinner, laughing and talking. But as it nears midnight, I physically wince as my pain meds wear off and my stitches throb.

"You okay?" Alex asks.

I nod slowly. "Just my head. I think I better get to bed."

He glances at his watch. "Shit. I've kept you up way too late."

Alec pulls me to my feet and gives me a hug. "Thanks for the company. You...this was fun."

"It was," I say. "Thanks for dinner."

We pause awkwardly. I want to kiss him, but my head is screaming at me.

Alec senses this, I think. He kisses my cheek, and I walk him to the door.

"When you have a free night," I say, "let me know. I'd like to do this again."

Alec nods. "Me, too."

Chapter 15

I didn't fall asleep until close to dawn, and by the time I woke up, even though I was starving, I didn't have the energy to make anything. I plowed my way through an apple, some carrot sticks, and two bowls of cereal.

But my body is used to starch and fat. Sad but true. So when Alec calls and asks if I'm up for dinner again tonight, I start drooling.

He asks me what I feel like eating, and I hem and haw. I'm trying to think of something Chinese that sounds good to my empty stomach, but the only thing that flashes through my brain is CHEESEBURGER.

He laughs. "I can do a mean cheeseburger."

So we're sitting on my back patio, the burgers on the grill, sipping hot chocolate. Hey, it's cold outside, and coffee's been burning a hole in my belly lately. Chocolate sounded perfect, and Alec graciously agreed to appease me.

"Do you need another blanket?" he asks as he notices me shiver.

I shake my head.

"Are you sure? We can move inside."

"I'm not cold, Alec," I say.

"But you're shaking. I can see it from here."

I laugh. "That's because you're here. And you make me nervous."

He rears back. "I'm sorry. I didn't mean to—"

"It's not anything you're doing," I say. "Well, it is. You're nice and smart and thoughtful. And you rescued me. And we have a ton of things in common. And I keep thinking about you walking into my room, and I wasn't wearing anything apart from that stupid cap, which we won't mention. 'Cause when I think about it, my hair is perfect and long and brushed, and I look beautiful, and you just cross the room and take me."

Alec just stares at me.

"So that's why I'm shaking. I want to touch you so badly I have to sit on my hands to keep myself from mauling you."

He smiles and lowers his eyes to his mug. "I was raised in a very Christian household, did I tell you that?"

"No."

"I met my ex-wife at church. She was my first."

"And how many have there been since?" I ask.

He shakes his head. "None."

"That was me," I say. "Married my first everything. But I've dated since. I get it."

"I don't have reservations," he says. "I mean, I'm not saving myself. I just haven't met anyone."

"Are you nervous?"

"Not with you." And then he laughs. "That's not entirely true. My wife wasn't very adventurous. I think I'm way behind the curve."

I sit back in my chair and sip my hot chocolate. "Is there something you've always wanted to try but never have?"

Alec ducks his head. "It's embarrassing. But in the interest of honesty...I've never given nor received oral sex."

I blink. "That sucks."

We both laugh.

"How's your head?" he asks.

"I'm riding the codeine," I say, "and I never thought I'd say that. This is the last day I'll take it, though."

Alec holds out a hand, and I slip mine in his, and he pulls me to my feet.

My shivers intensify. The look in his eyes...he's thinking about going down on me. And boy, do I want him to.

We're just holding hands and staring into each other's eyes. Neither of us makes a move.

"I'm going to kiss you," he whispers, but he still doesn't move.

I just nod lamely.

His fingers start to caress mine. He brings my hand to his mouth and kisses my palm. Then he slides my middle finger into his mouth and sucks on it.

Wah. I never knew that felt so good. I close my eyes, and I feel the suction of his lips, the tickling graze of his tongue, his warm mouth…

He reaches with his other hand for my cheek. He trails his fingers down the side of my face and traces my lips. I open them, and he puts his thumb in my mouth.

I suck. I lick. And his eyelids lower, and he shifts his stance, but still, he doesn't move closer.

I shudder, and my clit tingles.

And suddenly, he's on me. Alec's entire body is pressed to mine, and he welds his lips to mine, and our tongues dance. He cradles my cheeks in his hands as he worships my mouth.

"God, you taste good," he says as he trails his lips down to my neck and sucks the tender skin at my throat.

"Take me to the bedroom," I say.

We stumble all the way there, our mouths locked.

Alec lifts me by the waist and sets me on the edge of my bed. He slides my jeans and underwear off and tosses them to the floor. Then he pushes both my shirt and bra up and puts his lips around my nipple.

"Ahh," I say, cradling his head to my chest. He gives me the edge of his teeth, scraping them gently across the swollen flesh.

His fingers find my clit. He rubs it in circles while mercilessly biting my nipple. My thighs tremble and I start to pant.

He pushes me backward and pulls my ass to the very edge of the mattress.

"Guide me," he says, and then his mouth is on me.

"Lick my clit," I say. "A little to the left."

He laughs against me, and his tongue goes flat, and he licks upward, pulling on my clit with a long, steady swipe. And again. Another slow lick. Fuck, he's killing me!

"Faster," I say, and he speeds up. He traces a finger through my folds as he licks, and then he slides his index finger inside me and presses his thumb to my perineum. He rubs that delicious space above my ass while he pumps his finger, and his tongue flicks, and I'm seeing stars.

"Oh, God, I'm close," I say. "So close. There. Don't stop."

And suddenly my orgasm hits, and I cry out, and he continues to rub and pump his finger, and then he puts his lips around my clit and sucks on it.

Another orgasm hits, right on the heels of the first. I scream, and he sucks, and I try to move, but he has my legs pinned, and all I can do is ride the pleasure.

And then I laugh. Alec lifts his head with a grin, and I just laugh.

"Did you come?" he asks.

Ha.

I hold up two fingers. "Twice. I can't believe it. I've never done that."

He frowns. "Only twice?"

I sit up on my elbows. "Only twice? Twice is amazing!"

"I read where that technique can produce five orgasms, minimum," he says, shaking his head. "I must have done it wrong."

I nod my head. "I think you're right. You really should do it again. Give it a little more effort this time."

He looks at me suspiciously, and then he laughs. "So that was good for you?"

I tug him up to me and he crawls up on the bed, wrapping his arms around me.

"I want to return the favor so badly," I say. "I just don't think I can yet."

Alec kisses my nose and looks down at me. "I wouldn't let you. Heal first. It'll give me something to look forward to."

"Thank you," I say. "I…"

"You what?" he asks.

I sigh. "I just think you're really special. I feel lucky that we met."

He pulls me onto his chest and rubs a hand up and down my arm. "Me, too, Hope. Me, too."

⅋

We forgot about the burgers. Charred little hockey pucks, they were.

We ate them anyway.

Chapter 16

I don't exactly blow Nick off, but I tell him what happened, that I'm recovering, and that I just can't deal with a relationship right now. He has the nerve to argue with me, saying I should have called him. Maybe I should have. Decent guy, I guess, if a little overwrought, but it just didn't happen.

Now I have Alec.

Okay, so we've been dating a week, and Christmas is in two days. I got presents from him just for being a klutz, so even though we haven't discussed it, I know we're exchanging presents. I just have to figure out what to get him.

So Martika and I are shopping.

"How about a tie?" she says. "Lawyers always need ties."

"I don't want to get him something he needs," I say. "He can buy a tie. I want to get him something he'd never buy for himself."

"Have you slept with him yet?"

I shake my head. "It's weird. I want to sleep him, maybe more than I've ever wanted to sleep with anyone. But I love the fact that we haven't. I haven't even seen his body yet. I just feel all gooey when I'm with him."

Martika laughs. "It's only been a week. You can't expect that feeling to last."

"I know. After Matt, God knows I know. But I'm enjoying it."

"You should," she says, bumping her shoulder into mine. "How about sex toys? That could spice things up."

"Were you listening?" I say with a laugh. "We're hot. We don't need any more spice."

"You could go the tame route," she says. "Massage oil, maybe a book of erotica to read aloud, a butt plug."

I stare at her. "On what planet is a butt plug tame?"

She grins. "Whoops. Guess I just shared a little too much. Benny always—"

"Stop. Don't tell me."

Martika laughs. "How about the *Kama Sutra*? You could try out a different position every night."

I smile. "That's...intriguing."

"Ah. I found something you like. Let's go to that sex shop on Tustin Avenue. You probably don't even know all the possibilities." She takes my arm and steers me in the direction of our car.

"I don't know," I say. "I've never been to one of those places. Maybe I can just browse on the Internet."

She stops and looks at me. "You've never been to a sex shop?"

I shake my head, and she smiles.

"Excellent. A virgin."

ဆ

Bed Knobs and Broomsticks is a store I've passed a hundred times and never knew existed. In the center of a run-down strip mall, it looks like it's vacant—the windows are blacked out, and the neon lettering of the sign is broken, just the first B flickering on and off with a loud hum.

"I think they're closed," I say, but Martika just drags me by the arm with a roll of her eyes.

She opens the door and insists I go in first. Right.

Holy Mary Mother of Joseph.

The place is packed. I look back to the parking lot, not that I can see it through the blackened windows, and I swear there were only two cars in the lot. Where did everyone park?

A young girl with a nose piercing bounces over to us. "Welcome!" she says, handing us each a flyer. "Christmas sale. Two-for-one on all dildos, the pony play accessories are 50% off, and crotchless panties are buy one get two free. Lots of other deals. Let me know if you need any help."

"Oooh," Martika says. "Crotchless panties. Thanks!"

I smile weakly, and the girl moves on.

"What's pony play?" I whisper to Martika.

She grins. "Nothing you'd be interested in. Unless you want to prance around like a horse while Alec pulls on your pony tail and whips your ass with a crop."

My eyes widen. "That's a thing?"

"Don't you watch porn?"

I giggle. "Apparently I've been watching the wrong kind."

"Let's look at the lingerie," she says, and I follow her. "That's pretty tame."

Except nothing in this store is tame.

I wander over to a rack of corsets. I've never worn a corset. Except none of these have cups for your boobs, just cut-outs, so you're hanging in the wind. Some are leather, some shiny vinyl, one is a kind of tapestry print with silk ribbons that tie up the back. It's rather gorgeous, like something you'd see in a historical movie. Well, maybe a Victorian-era porn. Do they make those?

I check the price. Holy crap. It's $256.

"What do you think?" Martika is holding up a red vinyl body suit, two holes cut out for the nipples. And it's crotchless.

"I think it looks hot," I say. "I mean, like you'd sweat a lot."

She shrugs. "Sex makes you sweat anyway. If you're doing it right."

"Good point."

She sighs and puts it back on the rack. "I can't justify $500. Not even for great sex."

"Five hundred dollars?" I gulp.

"It's an investment in the relationship," she says. "That's how you have to look at these prices."

Apparently.

We find the crotchless panties, $32 each. But today you get three for that price.

Crotchless panties really defeat the purpose of panties at all. I almost dismiss them. But then I think, what if I were wearing a pair with a skirt? What if we went out to dinner, and I slid Alec's hand between my thighs, under the table? That could be fun.

I gravitate to the white, thinking that's what Alec would like. But white doesn't look good on me. You'd think being half Hispanic that my skin would be darker, but nope. I got my Mom's skin. I can tan, but I don't like to. Mom's skin, Dad's dark hair and eyes.

I look great in black. But black's so boring.

I choose a lacy hot pink.

"Pick two," I tell Martika. "My treat." She squeals and picks a shiny black vinyl and a red mesh pair.

Then we wander over to the toys.

Yikes. Half of this stuff…I have no idea what it's for. I'm completely embarrassed to be in here.

Martika feels none of that. She marches over to a display and grabs a giant red dildo.

"This sucker's heavy."

I lean into her ear. "Wouldn't that hurt? How the hell does that fit inside you?"

"Women's bodies are amazing, aren't they? If you can expel a baby, certainly you can accommodate this guy."

I cringe. "But why would you want to?"

She laughs and puts it back. "I forgot. Tame. Oh! How about this?" She picks up a box and flips it over. "A couples' massager."

It looks like a two-pronged clip. The picture on the box shows one end of the clip inserted into the woman, and the other end rests on her clit. Both ends vibrate.

"How is it for couples?" I ask.

She points to the last picture. "You use it during sex. The guy slips right in above this prong, and he gets the vibrations, too. Sounds fun."

I stare at the picture. "Wouldn't it hurt?"

She hands me the box and picks up the massager on display. "Feel it. It's wrapped in that rubbery silicone. If you lube it up, I don't think you'd feel it at all."

I continue to read the box. It suggests that a woman could wear the massager all day long, with no one the wiser. There's even a phone app you can download to discreetly change the vibration settings.

I imagine that, wearing the massager while I go about my day. I wonder how many women do this kind of thing and I never noticed.

"What do you think?" Martika asks.

"It's interesting," I say, "but it's a little early in the relationship."

"Get it for you," she says. "Do you even have a vibrator?"

My cheeks burn. "No."

"What color? I'm buying it for you for Christmas. Use it alone, and when you're ready, you can share it with Alec."

"Martika."

"Hope."

I stare at her. I kind of want it. Just to see.

"I'll buy it," I say. I choose the purple one, of course. "Now, let's focus. I need to find something for Alec."

I choose some massage oil that smells like margaritas and tastes like lime. Supposedly. I also choose some lubricant, a book of erotica, and a book on fellatio. I think I'm pretty well versed, but since Alec has never experienced it, it can't hurt me to brush up on my technique.

We wait in a twenty-minute line, and when we finally get to the register, I'm dying. Every time the door opens, I expect to see someone I know and be caught. I just want to pay and get out.

"Oooh, you chose the couples' massager," the girl says loudly with a grin. "It's awesome. You're gonna love it."

"Great," I mumble. And then to my horror, she starts opening the package.

"There are no returns on these," she says. "I mean, how gross would that be, right?" She takes the purple clip out of the box. "Have you used one before?"

I shake my head.

"It comes with about ten minutes of charge, just enough so we can prove it works. Be sure to plug it in as soon as you get home. Once charged, it should be good to go for a few hours. Now, this is the end you stick inside your vagina. It comes with ten different speeds, and ten different pulses. Here, hold on to it, and I'll show you."

I can't believe this. At least ten people are waiting behind me, listening to this entire exchange. Martika has to take my hand and place it on the insertable end.

"Touch this button once to turn it on. Press it to change the pulse. This is the continuous vibrate...and this is the cha-cha-cha...the sine wave...the—"

"I get it," I say, snatching my hand back.

"Obviously, you can't press the buttons while it's inside you, so that's why they have a phone app. Do you want me to demonstrate it?"

"No. I can figure it out."

"Great! So we know it works. Here's a sheet for tips on keeping your toys clean. I'll just put it in your bag. You know, it works great for a man, too. Slip this end in his anus, and rest the other at the base of his penis. He'll love it."

Martika is snickering next to me. I finally get to pay, and we get the hell outta there.

And as we step into the sunlight outside, she bursts out laughing.

"Your face," she says. "You should have seen your face."

I glare at her. And then I burst out laughing, too.

Chapter 17

Alec has an older sister who is married with two young kids. According to Alec, she did everything right—graduated top of her class at Berkeley, spent five years at Ernst & Young, married a nice church-going Chinese boy who is now a thoracic surgeon—and yet it still wasn't good enough for his parents. When they passed away, she quit her job, got a tattoo, and became a stay-at-home mom and part-time graphic artist. She still has to hide the tattoo from her in-laws, but her husband loves her anyway.

Alec also has a large extended family, and they always get together on Christmas Eve. He asked me to join them, and though my stomach's in knots, I accepted.

"So tell me what to expect," I say as he drives us to his aunt's house in Pasadena.

"There will be at least sixty people there, I told you that, I think," he says, and I nod. "Don't let it overwhelm you. My aunts will be very accommodating and doting. Guests are important to them. They'll ply you with food and drink, so just thank them and take what they offer, and if you've had enough or if there's something you don't like, just pass it to me."

I smile at him. "Thanks."

He smiles back. "It's just a bunch of us sitting around catching up. But my aunts always insist on singing Christmas carols. My sister will dutifully play the piano, bitching under her breath the entire time."

I laugh. "I love Christmas carols. I can do that. I can even play if she doesn't want to."

He glances at me. "I thought you just played guitar."

"Guitar, piano, bass...I played the harmonica for a while, but I like to sing more. You know I've messed around with the clarinet. And I can do some drums."

"You're a one-woman band. How come you haven't played for me yet?"

"Because it's only been a week. Maybe I'll play for you tonight."

He grins. "So are you gonna tell me what's in the bag?" He points to the large Macy's bag at my feet.

"Gifts. I brought gifts for the kids, and one for your aunt. You said she collects antiques, right?"

Alec reaches a hand out and squeezes my thigh. "That was really thoughtful. You didn't have to do that."

"I wanted to. But I admit, I'm nervous."

"Don't be. They'll love you."

∽

Auntie Ju-Ju greets us warmly with hugs and bows.

"You are lovely!" she says, taking my hand and patting it. "So lovely."

"What a beautiful home," I say, and I mean it. It's an historical Victorian, with oriental rugs, velvet settees, and Ming Dynasty vases. I only know this because I got a mini introduction to antiques when I went shopping for her gift.

"Oh," she says, waving a dramatic hand. "Such junk. Everything old. Like me!"

I laugh. I know she's only around 60, and if it weren't for her graying hair, she'd look like she's in her forties.

Alec leads me to the parlor-turned-family room, where a couple is sitting on the couch, two kids at their feet.

"Jane," he says, and the woman looks up and smiles. She pops to her feet and gives Alec a hug.

"Thank God," she says. "Someone normal. Sort of." She pokes him in the stomach with a smile. "Auntie Betty is driving me crazy."

"I want you to meet Hope," he says, turning to me and taking my hand. "Hope, this Jane, and this is her husband Ernie, and their kids, Ryan and Faith."

I shake Jane's hand, then Ernie's. "It's nice to meet you."

She raises her arms to the ceiling. "Hallelujah! You chose a white girl. Us Chinese, we're crazy."

I just stare at her, and Alec sighs.

Jane laughs. "I'm kidding. Sort of. Alec's ex-wife was fresh off the boat and madder than a hatter. Buy American. That's the advice, isn't it?"

"Uh…" I have no idea what to say to that.

Jane links her arm through mine. "I'm kidding. Sort of. Ignore me. Ernie's been in surgery for forty-eight hours, and I've been stuck with the kids. It's made me loopy. Let's get you a drink."

She starts to lead me away, and I look back at Alec.

He smiles. "She's kidding. Lighten up, Jane. I actually want Hope to speak to me tomorrow."

Jane just laughs.

&

Jane pours us each a glass of champagne, and we wind through groups of people, her giving me quick introductions, me remembering none of them. We finally settle on a bench in the perfectly manicured English garden out back, and Jane gives me a long look.

"So how long have you and Ernie been married?" I ask.

"Twelve years. Took me ten before I appreciated him, but now, I'm hooked."

"I want that trick," I say. "Isn't it usually the other way around?"

She smiles ruefully. "I was an asshole as a teenager. My head was so far up my father's ass I couldn't see straight. He barked, and I jumped. I picked Ernie for him. Then I had to grow up and figure out what was good for me. I'm blessed that Ernie was that thing."

"That is lucky," I say, and she nods.

"How did you and Alec meet?" she asks.

"I needed an estate attorney, and he was referred to me by a colleague."

"Oooh," she says, a wicked gleam in her eye. "Dating the client. Nice."

I smile. "We just connected. I've only known him a couple of weeks, but it feels like longer."

Jane swallows some champagne and leans back against the bench. "Did he tell you about his marriage?"

"A bit," I say.

"He deserves someone nice. Someone with her shit together. I swear, he'd be ruling the world by now if she hadn't held him back."

"It was that bad, huh?"

She nods. "I won't spill details, but...yeah. He twisted himself in knots trying to please her, trying to fix her. But enough about that. Do you babysit?"

I laugh. "Never have. Are you trying to recruit me?"

"Absolutely," she says. "I'm giving Ernie a ski trip for Christmas. We desperately need some alone time. Maybe you could help Alec out."

I raise an eyebrow. "Alec is keeping the kids?"

"Yep. Four days. The guy's a saint. I give him a hard time, but honestly...he's a great guy, Hope. His crazy family not withstanding."

I smile. "I think his family's pretty great. No complaints."

Jane laughs. "Wait until you meet Uncle Harold, Betty's husband."

"Alec said we'll probably sing carols later. And that you have to play the piano?"

She rolls her eyes. "That's why I'm on my fourth glass of champagne. It's painful."

"I can play if you don't want to."

She eyes me. "You play?"

I nod.

She stands up. "Excellent. Let's go take a test run."

ॐ

We sit side-by-side at the grand piano. It must be over a hundred years old, but it's polished to perfection, and the ivory keys show no signs of chipping. Either it doesn't get a lot of use, or Auntie Ju-Ju is meticulous.

"Let's start easy," she says. "*Silent Night.*"

That's one of my favorites. I close my eyes, set the tune in my head, adding a few flourishes here and there just to show off, and then I play. I get lost in the music. At some point, Jane slips off the bench, but I finish the song.

And suddenly the entire house seems to burst into applause.

I open my eyes and turn around. The room is crammed with people, and they're all applauding.

"*The First Noel*!" someone yells.

Tears sting my eyes. I don't know why.

Then Alec sits beside me. "Do you know it? *The First Noel*?"

My throat is too tight to speak, so I nod. I set the tune…and I play.

Alec's pitchy voice, low, is in my ear. It makes me smile.

And then the entire room is singing. I join in.

For two hours, I sing and I play.

❧

Most of the family has left by the time Auntie Ju-Ju, Auntie Betty, and Uncle Harold insist on one last drink. I suddenly remember my gift, and Alec grabs it from the foyer and sets it in Auntie Ju-Ju's lap.

"For me?" she says. "Oh no, oh no. Not for me!"

"Alec told me you love antiques," I say. "I went to the antique mall in Old Towne Orange, and the clerk helped me pick this out. She said you'd love it."

She tears open the paper and carefully opens the box. Nestled inside a bunch of packing peanuts is an Ansonia mantle clock, circa 1897.

Alec and Harold both gasp. Auntie Betty looks away. Ju-Ju just looks speechless.

"She didn't know," Alec says, but Auntie Ju-Ju waves him off.

"Shush, you! Beautiful! My, my. I never had such beauty in my home before! Ansonia is old and expensive. Very expensive." She rummages in her pocket and pulls out a penny, holding it out to me. I look at Alec, and he nods his head. So I take the penny.

"I put it here, above the fireplace," Ju-Ju declares, placing the clock front and center. "Where all can see."

Alec is fighting a smile. I don't get it.

"What?"

"Alec, you a good boy," Ju-Ju says, "so shut up. Now. Let's drink."

∞

As soon as we get in the car, I turn to Alec. "What was with the clock?"

He smiles. "A clock is just about the worst gift you can give to the Chinese," he says. "The word for clock sounds like the word for death. You basically told her her time was short and she was going to die."

My mouth hangs open.

Alec laughs. "But she didn't care. She loved it. And she loved you, or she would never have put that clock out."

"You're telling me I just insulted the matriarch of your family?"

"Pretty much."

My eyeballs burn, and I blink hard.

"Hey. Are you crying?"

I stare out the passenger window. "No."

"Hope, it's fine. You didn't know, and she's lived here for thirty years. You gave her a beautiful gift, and that's exactly how she took it."

I try to nod, just to see if it will make me feel better. It doesn't.

"What was with the penny?" I finally manage.

"She was buying the gift from you, so that it wasn't a gift anymore. That way, she wasn't subject to the death implications."

"I'm sorry," I say. "Insulting her was the last thing on my mind."

Alec pulls up to a stoplight and looks at me. "Hope, everyone knows that. You have nothing to feel bad about."

"Uncle Harold wouldn't even say goodbye to me. I guess that's why."

"He's a fruitcake, and he's not even Chinese," Alec says. "He's Jewish. And I'm sure Auntie Betty has lots of stories about Harold trying to fit into our family and failing."

I sniff. "Would you ask her?"

We both laugh.

"You know," he says, "this is kind of a turn-on."

"Me insulting your family?"

He shakes his head. "You crying. I mean, not the actual crying, but you so upset because you care that much about my family."

I finally look at him. "My crying doesn't bother you?"

"I don't want you to feel bad," he says, "but no. Why would your crying bother me? That's like saying your laughter bothers me. It's a part of you."

ॐ

Alec drops me off at my mom's so I can wake up with her Christmas morning. He gives me a long kiss, his fingers entwining with mine and holding tight.

And when he tries to leave, I won't let go of his hand.

So we sit on the front step, my head on his shoulder, and we talk. And when it's two AM, I finally let him go home.

Chapter 18

New Year's Day, I have coffee and watch the Rose Parade with my mother and then brunch with Martika and Benny. Martika's finally starting to show, just a bit in her lower tummy, enough that she can't button the top of her jeans. And she's a healthy eater normally, but the baby has other ideas. I'm in awe as I watch her plow through an omelet larger than her plate, an entire side of hash browns, and eight pieces of bacon.

I'll give her a pass on the bacon.

And then I head to Alec's. A date with his niece and nephew.

We haven't seen each other since Christmas Eve, even though we've talked every day. I woke up Christmas morning with the flu, and Alec was working overtime so that he could take four days off to watch the kids, and then Martika and Benny and I and a few others had bought tickets months ago to a New Year's Eve Rolling Stones concert. I was perfectly ready to give up my ticket, but Alec had poker night planned with his friends, so I went.

I still have Alec's presents in my car. But I'm thinking that today, with the kids about, wouldn't be the appropriate time to give them to him.

He has a gorgeous home in Old Towne Orange, close to his office and about five miles from me. It's a craftsman-style bungalow, meticulous in every detail. It's one of those houses that you drive by and itch to see the inside.

Four-year-old Faith opens the door when I knock.

"Uncle!" she yells. "She's here!"

I step inside and crouch down. "Hi, Faith. It's nice to see you again." I notice Alec and Ryan enter the room.

"Take your shoes off," she says, sticking a finger in her ear. "They go there." She points to a shoe rack next to the door.

"Right," I say. "Thanks for the tip." She smiles as I stand, and I slip my flats off and put them in a shoe cubby. Faith is staring at my feet.

"Your toes are purple," she says.

I wiggle them. "Yep. Would you like purple toes?"

"Daddy has a purple toe," she says. "I dropped a soup on it."

"You dropped a soup?"

She nods, and Alec laughs. He comes to me and gives me a hug.

"A can of soup," he says. "You dropped a can of soup on his toe."

"That's what I said," Faith says.

I cringe. "Ouch."

"Let me take your coat," Alec says, easing it off my shoulders. He also takes my purse and hangs them both on the hall tree. Then he claps his hands together. "So. I'm fixing lunch, and then I thought we'd go to the park. Any objections?"

Six-year-old Ryan pumps a fist in the air. "The park. Yes!"

"Will you push me on the swing?" I ask.

Alec grins and leans in my ear. "That sounds like foreplay."

"What's foreplay?" Faith asks, and my eyes go wide.

"I said four days," Alec lies, ruffling her hair. "Come on. The sooner you eat, the sooner we get to play."

Alec has made peanut butter and jelly sandwiches. The kids have impeccable manners. I notice they both place their napkins in their laps, although neither one of them uses the napkin. Ryan wipes his mouth on his sleeve between bites, and Faith doesn't seem to notice the peanut butter on her nose or the jelly on her chin.

"Let me give you a tour while the kids eat," Alec says. He takes my hand and leads me around. "Guest bath. And this is my office. Three bedrooms total, so I pilfered one for work. This is the spare bedroom—never had any use until now. And this is the master."

I walk into Alec's bedroom. He has a mission-style bedroom suite, which fits the house.

A plush black velvet comforter tops the bed. Everything's neat and tidy and perfectly in place.

"Do you actually live like this, or did you clean up for me?" I ask.

He laughs. "A bit of both. I'm generally neat, but not this neat."

"Do you have a maid?"

He nods. "Once a week. I could do it myself, but I just don't have time."

"Same here," I say. And then I laugh. "Actually, now that I don't have a job, I do have the time."

"Have you thought about it?" he asks. "Suing them?"

"I'm not gonna do that," I say. "I'm taking it as a sign. I've wanted to pursue my music for a long time, and now I don't have an excuse not to."

"I can't wait to hear you play the guitar," he says. "If you're better at that than you are at the piano...wow."

"There are a million talented musicians out there," I say. "I'm not that special."

Alec grips my arms. "Don't say that. Don't create obstacles for yourself. You're amazing. A-mazing. Believe in yourself."

I lean forward and take his mouth with mine. Alec sighs into the kiss and puts his arms around me. I run my hands down his back, feeling the strained muscles, and then I grip his ass tight.

He laughs. "God, I can't believe we have to wait four days."

My erect nipples are rubbing against my bra, and my underwear's now uncomfortably damp.

"Me, either."

ဆ

The park. I haven't been to the park since I was a kid.

As soon as we hit the grass, the kids run ahead of us to the jungle gym. Alec wraps an arm around my waist and sighs.

"I love this," he says. "I don't do this enough."

"Relax, you mean?"

He nods. "I run, and I get to the gym most days, but I don't really get outside and just enjoy the day."

"I started taking walks after my divorce," I say. "I'd get up early, before the sun was even up, and there's a smell to the air. You can predict the weather based on that smell. And you realize how loud the day is when you get up early. No gardeners blowing leaves, no cars honking. Sometimes I miss silence."

We settle on a bench near the play area where we can keep an eye on the kids.

"What's your perfect life?" Alec asks. "Describe for me a day in that life."

I smile. "An early-morning walk with my husband. Doesn't have to be long, maybe twenty or thirty minutes, but just some time to connect in that silence. Coffee, news, maybe splitting a bagel. And then the kids get up, all of them, lots of them, and I help dress them and brush teeth and sing songs, and I get tight hugs and sloppy kisses from the whole lot, even the teenagers...then work. Writing songs. Recording. Whatever I need to do. Laundry, I'd imagine. Then homework and watching the kids play sports and music and acting in plays, and kissing boo-boos and telling them that yes, that Sophie is a mean bitch and you have my permission to ignore her...and a loud family dinner, all of us, together. Then bath time and story time and snuggles...then a beer with my husband, a bath together, a couple hours of making love and touching and whispers...and then sleep. Glorious sleep."

Alec looks away, and I frown.

"Did I say something wrong?"

He turns back to me, and his eyes are shiny. "You just described my perfect life."

⁂

We get the kids down for bed. Only took four readings of *Goodnight Moon* and five repetitions of the theme song to *Mickey Mouse's Clubhouse*.

We settle on the couch with coffee, and Alec pulls a present from the side of the couch.

"I know it's late, but Merry Christmas," he says.

"I have your presents in the car, but I want you to wait to open them."

"Why?" he asks.

"We need to be alone."

Alec grins. "I can wait. But you have to open this now."

I slide the gold ribbon off the small package and tear off the wrapping. I lift the lid of the box.

Inside is a business card.

I pick it up. *Joseph Kirshner - Producer, Lockstep Records.*

"Look on the back," he says. So I flip the card over.

January 18, 10 AM, my office is written in block letters.

I look up. "You know Joseph Kirshner?"

"We were frat brothers at Penn," Alec says. "He wants to meet with you."

"Lockstep Records," I say, the card trembling in my hand. "You believe in me that much?"

"More," he says. "But this is the best I could do."

"Alec…to call in a favor, from a friend…"

"I didn't call in any favor," he says. "I showed him your video from that restaurant, and the one my sister took of you playing at Christmas. He requested the meeting. I didn't have anything to do with it."

I launch myself at him, peppering his face with kisses, and Alec laughs.

"Do you think we can make out?" I ask. "Just a little bit?"

He grins. "I thought you'd never ask."

Chapter 19

I spent all four days with Alec and Ryan and Faith. I fell in love with them. All of them.

There it is. I love Alec Chang.

It's been on the tip of my tongue to tell him. Every time he laughs, every time he frowns, every time he touches me...I want to shout it!

But I'm waiting for tonight. Finally...we'll be alone.

Alec doesn't finish with work his first day back to the office until after eight. He comes in my door dragging, his fingers clawing at the tie around his neck.

"Rough day?" I ask as I take his coat and jacket.

"Not rough, but long," he says. "Come here."

I nestle into him and give him a kiss. "Do you need a drink?"

"I probably shouldn't if my goal is to be wide-awake, but yes."

I pour us each a glass of wine. "Nerves?"

He shakes his head. "My cock has been hard since lunch just thinking about tonight. I swear everything took twice as long because I couldn't concentrate."

I laugh. Then I push his presents, sitting on the kitchen counter, toward him. "These might help."

He opens the massage oil and lube and grins. He opens the erotica and gulps. And then he gets to the last present.

I wrapped the couple's massager. Of course I charged it first and set up the app on my phone.

He stares at the box, and I can see it shaking in his hands.

"Interesting, don't you think?"

He looks up at me, his lips split in a smile. "Have you tried this?"

"Not with a partner."

"Are we...using this tonight?"

I shake my head. "Not tonight. First I'm gonna take care of you. And then you're gonna fuck me. And then we're gonna make love until we fall asleep."

80

I tell Alec to sit on the bed and watch. Then I stand in front of him.

I slowly unbutton my blouse, one button at a time. Alec watches me with hooded gaze, his eyes focused on my fingers.

I hold the shirt closed and slide it off my shoulders. He smiles.

And then I let the shirt drop. I'm not wearing a bra, and my 34 D cups spill into the cool air. Alec starts to rise, but I push him gently back down.

I turn my back to him and slide the skirt from my waist. I bend all the way forward and step out of the skirt. I look over my shoulder, and Alec's lips are parted, his breath coming faster.

I straighten up and face him. "Now you," I say.

His fingers go to the buttons on his own shirt, but I shake my head.

"Stop. Let me."

I move to him and work on the buttons. I watch his throat work as he swallows.

"Hope, you're so beautiful. I feel like I've waited a lifetime for this."

I grin. "It gets better."

He shakes his head. "I don't think it does."

I slide his shirt off and get a good look at him for the first time. He's perfectly toned, lean, and there's not a hair on his chest. I run my hands over the smooth skin. I can't believe this is mine. All mine.

I unbuckle his belt, undo his pants, and run my fingers over his stomach. The muscles contract, and he catches his breath.

Then I slide his pants and boxers down in one swift motion. His cock springs out and nearly slaps me in the face.

He steps out of his pants and laughs. "I think I need to lie down. My legs won't hold me up."

I get a great view of his smooth, tight ass as he climbs on the bed. I follow him up and lie down across his chest. He pulls me in and kisses me.

I melt into him, my tits pressed against his hard nipples, his tongue swirling against mine. I nibble at his lips, and my hands roam, until I've got one wrapped tight around his cock. It's so smooth, hardened velvet, and it swells in my hand.

"I'm not gonna last if you do that," he says. "I've been ready to come since breakfast."

I laugh and slide down between his legs. "You don't have to last. Don't worry about how long it takes, and don't hold back. Just go with it."

Alec leans back into the pillows. "You want directions?"

I slide my hand down his cock and grip the base tight, giving it a squeeze. "If you want it to be good, hell yes."

He laughs, and I open my mouth and take him in. The laugh turns to a gasp.

I run my tongue along the rim of the head and then down the length of his cock. I get it all nice and slicked up, and then I concentrate on the head, sucking on it gently in a pulsing rhythm.

Andrea Ring

His cock hardens some more. I didn't think that was possible.

Then I pump my mouth over him, up and down. I manage to get about three quarters of it down my throat with every stroke, and I use my hand to rub the bottom, twisting it on every upstroke. Alec's hips start to buck along with me.

I have a free hand, so I swirl my finger in my saliva and rub it around the rim of his ass.

Alec groans. "Fuck, Hope. Oh my God. Harder."

I suck harder. I grip harder. I taste that sweet salty bit of pre-come as Alec climbs, and I flick my tongue on the spot where the head of his cock meets the shaft. Alec twitches, and I laugh against him.

"I'm close," he says. "Faster."

I bob my head faster, loving every minute of this, every moan and twitch and gasp making my nipples harder, my pussy wetter, until Alec shoves a hand in my hair and grips tight.

"Yes, Hope. Yes! Oh, God!" And he unloads a mouthful, and I swallow it all eagerly, and I lick and suck until he calms done and his balls loosen.

I finally lift my head, and Alec lifts his. "Kiss me," he says.

I lie on top of him and ravish his mouth. He flips me over onto my back and locks his lips around my nipple. I hold his head to my chest. I can already feel his cock growing hard again against my thigh.

I'm on the pill, and Alec knows this. Nothing to be awkward about now.

"You said I'm gonna fuck you first, right?" he asks, his hands still caressing my thighs.

I nod.

"On all fours."

I grin. I climb to my knees and thrust my ass in the air. One of his hands massages it, squeezing and rubbing, while the other rubs his cock over my pussy lips.

And then he's inside me.

He pumps his hips, and I thrust backward to meet him. He reaches forward and finds my clit with his fingers, rubbing in circles while he fucks me.

"Alec," I breathe. I pull a pillow under my chest and hold it tight. Alec speeds up, pumping into me hard and fast, so hard I have to fight to catch my breath.

"Don't stop," I say. "Yes."

My ass slaps hard against his groin. I feel his cock to the tips of my toes. My entire body tingles, and my arms shake.

"Go, Hope," he says, bending forward to kiss the small of my back. "Let go."

I reach a hand between us and place it on top of his. We both rub my clit, and my orgasm bursts, and I cry out, my pussy muscles clamping down hard on him.

Alec groans. And then he pumps into me twice, hard, and collapses against my back.

My knees give out, and my cheek buries itself in the pillow. Alec licks my ass and gives it a sweet kiss.

"I can't move," I say, and we both laugh.

He falls down beside me, and we stare into each other's eyes.

"I never thought I'd have this," he says. "It doesn't seem real."

"I know," I say. "I feel the same way."

"Hope." And then he places his hands on my cheeks. "I'm in love with you."

I flip to my back and sigh. "Damn it!"

Alec sits up in alarm. "Damn it?"

"I wanted to say it first!" I turn back to him, and he laughs. I run the back of my fingers over his forehead, down his cheek, over his lips. "Alec, I love you."

And then we kiss. And explore. And discover.

We love.

Chapter 20

Dr. Steinburg gives me a hug when I enter his office. I have a goofy grin on my face, and he smiles at me.

"I know my hugs are golden, but I'm sensing something else is at work here."

I flop back on the couch. "I'm in love."

He chuckles. "Wow."

"I know," I say. "It's been about a month, but I found him. He's everything I want."

"Tell me."

"He's an attorney," I say. "He has a loud, messy international family, which is interesting. He's Chinese, and none of his Chinese aunts—seven of them—married someone from their own culture. His dad's family were missionaries, and they grew up in Indonesia, South Africa, different parts of Asia, so they married men from all over the place. His parents passed away, but he's still close with the rest of the family, most of whom immigrated here. He has grandparents in Beijing."

"You've met the family?" he asks.

"At Christmas. I made a major cultural faux pas, but they were gracious about it. I loved them."

"That's a challenge in itself," he says. "Meeting the family. And to have cultural differences, doubly so."

"I still have a lot to learn, I think, about their culture, but Alec was born here. He's not that different from me."

Dr. Steinburg nods. "Tell me more."

"He's kind," I say. "Intelligent. Sexy. And he's comfortable with my feelings. I cried when I accidentally insulted his aunt, and it didn't bother him at all."

"And how does he feel about your music?"

"Completely supportive," I say. "And he kept his niece and nephew overnight for four days when his sister went on a trip, and he's amazing with them. He wants a family, just like me."

"He sounds wonderful," Dr. Steinburg says. "And have you told him about your childhood?"

"He knows who my dad is and how he treated us. I haven't given explicit details, though."

"And have you come across anything that would give you pause? I don't want you to pick at the relationship, but I also don't want you to ignore any warning signs."

"He does work a lot," I say. "He runs his own firm, so he has to, but it's nothing abnormal or unhealthy. He's really neat. I mean, I'm not a dirtbag, but I'm not as neat as he is. And he's pretty serious, but I like that."

"You mentioned that his dad's family were missionaries," he says. "Is he religious?"

I nod. "That's how he was raised, but he doesn't go to church much. Just holidays, mostly."

"And you're okay raising your children with his faith?"

I shrug. "I haven't thought about it."

"A month is a little early, perhaps, but I'm sensing you're all in. If this moves fast, you'll need to have that discussion."

I nod.

"How does your mother feel about him?"

I sigh. "She met him briefly, but that was before we started dating. I think she's avoiding getting to know him. She's still peeved at me that I gave her the house."

Dr. Steinburg nods again. Since Mom sees him every week, he probably knows more about her thoughts on the matter than I do.

"I'm gonna try to pin her down this weekend," I say.

"Does Alec know about our sessions?" he asks.

"No."

"Does he know you have brain damage?"

"No."

"Does he know you can't have children biologically?"

I shift on the couch. "I can have children biologically."

"Does he know you shouldn't?"

"I don't know that," I say. "You don't know that. No one does."

Dr. Steinburg stares at me. I stare back.

"Why do you think you cannot acknowledge that you live with a heart defect?"

"I acknowledge it," I say. "It was corrected before I turned one, and it hasn't affected me since."

"And when was the last time you saw your cardiologist?"

"I go annually," I say. "Last March, I think. I've never had a problem."

"Hope." Dr. Steinburg leans forward and throws his legal pad on the table between us. "Stop this. Talk to me. I know you're not this obtuse."

I press my lips together. "My mother had no right to talk to you about this. I'm not discussing it."

"Ignoring it won't make it go away," he says. "I've done some research, and based on what your mother has said—"

"My mother doesn't know what she's talking about!" I yell. "She hasn't gone to the doctor with me since I was 14! I can have children!"

"At what cost?" he asks softly.

Tears well in my eyes, and I choke on a sob. "Do you...do you know what's it like? I had a shitty childhood, and that's putting it mildly. I have visible lesions in my brain...brain damage so bad that I...I had to learn how to write my name again when I was 10. And now...I'm living. Trying to live. And you want me to face the possibility that I...my adulthood will be as shitty as my childhood? That my aortic valve is going to leak...I'll have open heart surgery, and a mechanical valve, and...I can't. I can't think about it. I don't want to think about it."

Dr. Steinburg gets up and sits next to me on the couch. He puts his arms around me, and I sob into his chest.

He doesn't speak.

And the only reason I can think of for that is that he has nothing comforting to say.

Chapter 21

I spend my days polishing the songs I want to play for Joseph Kirshner. I choose the ones that best represent me and the kind of album I'd like to produce. Bluesy, a little bit folksy, stripped down and raw. Kind of like Tori Amos with a guitar instead of a piano.

Alec finally has an early evening available, and I set up dinner with Martika and Benny. They haven't met him yet, and I'm dying for them all to meet. I just hope Martika doesn't embarrass me too much.

I get home after running some errands, and start a load of laundry. My doorbell rings.

I yank it open, and there's Matt.

"Hey," he says. "Happy New Year."

I hang on the edge of the door, blocking his entrance. "Happy New Year."

He holds out a postcard. "This came in the mail for you. Guess they didn't update your address."

I stare at the appointment reminder card for my cardiologist. Why the fuck do these things pop up all at once?

"Thanks."

"How's the head?" he asks.

"Fine."

"I came to see you in the hospital," he says. "Did your Mom tell you?"

I blink. "No."

He smiles. "Figures. So no complications?"

I shake my head. I can't seem to tear my eyes away from the postcard.

"You okay?" he asks.

"I'm seeing someone." I finally lift my eyes to his. "He's great, and I love him, but I haven't told him about this."

Matt swallows hard. "You love him?"

I nod.

Matt looks away across the yard and shoves his hands in his pockets. "If he loves you, too, it won't make a difference."

"How do I say it? How do I tell him I might not...might not be able to have kids?"

Matt's eyes turn glassy, and he blinks hard. "You just say it. If he can't handle it, it's better to know now, right?"

I shake my head. "I can't handle it. How can I expect him to?"

Matt puts his arms around me. I don't hug him back, but I do bury my head in his chest and concentrate on breathing.

"If he can't handle it, fuck him," Matt says. "Stand up for yourself, Hope. Nothing is more important than your life."

He kisses my forehead and goes back to his car. I watch him until he's out of sight.

Matt gave up his ability to have kids for me. When he was just 24 years old, he got a vasectomy, insisting that my life was the most important thing. He said he was happy to adopt.

Except not a lot of agencies are willing to adopt kids out to a mother with a congenital heart defect and brain damage.

And now…I'm resigning Alec to the same sentence.

ଛ

We arrive at Martika and Benny's right on time. Martika hugs me and kisses my cheek, and then she pounces on Alec. "Welcome to the family!" she declares.

Family. Ha.

But Alec's all smiles.

Martika plies us with drinks, pours lemonade for herself, and we settle on the couch.

"Hope tells me you're expecting," Alec says. "When's the due date?"

"May fifth," Martika says, rubbing her belly. "We just found out yesterday we're having a boy."

I slosh my beer on my knee as I sit up too fast. "You are? You didn't tell me!"

"Congratulations!" Alec says, and he and Ben tap beer bottles.

"I knew I was seeing you tonight," Martika says. "Can you believe it? Benny gets the soccer goalie he's always wanted."

Acid burns in my throat. I feel like I might throw up.

Alec puts a hand on my knee. "You play soccer?" he asks Ben.

Benny nods. "Grew up with it. Played in college. There's a league down by Orange Coast College. The guys are intense. You play?"

Alec laughs. "Not since high school, but it sounds like fun."

"You should come out some time," Benny says. "You play any other sports?"

I excuse myself and go to the bathroom. I lock the door and lean on the counter, breathing deep.

"Hope?" Martika calls through the door. "You okay?"

I shake my head, not that she can see.

"Hope?"

I open the door. "I'm fine. I'm so happy for you. You know that, right?"

She takes my hand. "What's wrong?"

Then Alec and Benny come up behind her.

"There should be a law against this," Ben says. "Female powwows in the bathroom."

Martika ignores him. "Talk to me, Hope."

I raise my eyes to Alec. He suddenly catches on that something's wrong, and I see the concern in his eyes.

"I have a heart defect," I say. "It doesn't really affect me now, but my doctor says I'm looking at a valve replacement in the next ten years. I can have kids, I mean, I can get pregnant, but she thinks it would strain my heart too much."

Nobody moves.

"I'm sorry I didn't tell you," I say. "I didn't want to face it. But I've been incredibly selfish. I made you fall in love with me, and now you have to choose, me or kids. And that's so unfair. I'm not worth it."

Martika drops my hand and looks back at Ben. They both hightail it to the kitchen.

Alec turns and follows them. "Thanks for having us," he says to them. "I'm gonna take Hope home. I'll have her call you tomorrow."

He comes back to me, carrying my purse. I follow him to the car.

&

It's a silent drive. I feel numb. There are so many things I know I need to say, but I can't make my mouth open.

We get to my house, and Alec turns off his car and moves to open his door.

"You don't have to come in," I say. "I understand."

"What do you understand?" he asks.

"Why you have to go."

He opens his door. "Come on. Let's talk inside."

I sigh and follow him to the door.

We stand awkwardly in the foyer.

"It must be really hard to see Martika having a baby," he says.

"It wasn't before," I say. "I mean...I'm genuinely happy for her. But over the past couple of days, my heart condition was brought up, twice, and I'd forgotten about it. I hadn't thought about it in so long. And now it's all I can think about. I didn't mean to hide it from you, but there it was, in my mind, and I was feeling guilty for not telling you, and then I saw Martika, and—"

"Hope."

"What?"

"Take a breath." He moves to me and rubs his hands down my arms. "We went so fast. If you think about it, we haven't even been together two months."

"But if you had known from the beginning—"

"But I didn't," he says. "We can't go back. We can only deal with now."

I nod. "So…what are you thinking?"

"I'm not thinking," he says. "I'm feeling. I'm feeling protective."

I move away from him. "I don't want you to stay because you feel like you have to rescue me. I've been there in my last marriage, and all it does is create resentment."

"I'm a big boy," he says. "I take responsibility for my choices. I'd never blame you."

"You say that now, but what happens when you wake up one day, and you're forty, and we don't have kids, and I disgust you."

Alec frowns. "I knew you were self-deprecating, but I didn't know you hated yourself."

I have nothing to say to that.

"Tons of people can't have kids," he says. "Lots of them find love."

"But you want kids of your own," I say. "I know you do."

"Why are you pushing me away?" he asks.

"You're ignoring the other piece," I say. "I might die young. I have a 50% chance of developing Alzheimer's before I'm 50 because my dad knocked me around so much as a kid. Save yourself."

"Jesus!" he explodes. "The medical issues, we can deal with them. There are advances all the time. But your attitude is pissing me off!"

"I don't want to drag you down!" I scream back. "You don't deserve that!"

"I want you!" he says. "You! Hope Cruz, with all her neuroses, all her quirks, all her talent, even with her broken heart. I just want you!"

Tears spill from my eyes, and Alec takes me in his arms.

"You're a messy crier, you know that?"

A laugh bubbles out of my throat.

"I wouldn't have told you I love you if I didn't mean it," he says. "I meant it. I'm not going anywhere."

He kisses me. I gasp against his lips, trying to catch my breath, but there's no give in him. Alec kisses me hard and scoops me into his arms.

"Now I'm gonna show you," he says as he carries me to the bedroom.

Chapter 22

Lockstep Records is in the heart of LA, in a towering glass building. I ride the elevator to the thirtieth floor, where I spill into a waiting room that looks like it belongs in a law office. Except for the records and posters all over the walls. Can't picture those at Alec Chang & Associates.

Can't picture the goth girl behind the desk there, either. She's friendly, but the bullring through her nose is a little bit scary.

I don't know what I expected of Joseph Kirshner, but since he's friends with Alec, I guess I expected sedate. Professional. But he comes bounding into the waiting room in a red leather jacket and backwards ball cap, shooting a rubber band at someone behind him in the hallway.

"Bastard!" he yells with a laugh. "I'll get you next time!"

ॐ

The meeting doesn't go the way I expected it to, either.

Joseph insists on regaling me with stories of Alec in college, and while they're funny…I thought we were going to talk about music.

"He just sat there," Joseph says. "His skinny little hairless white legs dangling in the Jacuzzi, and that girl, rubbing her tits all over those legs…I think three of us banged her while he sat there."

Okay. That's one story I didn't need to hear.

"Anyway, you and Lockstep, it's a no-brainer. I have three songs looking for an artist, and they're poised to go to the top forty. Can you do pop?"

"Uh, what?"

"Pop music. You're a little old, but Carly Rae Jepsen pulled it off. With a little makeup and Botox, I think it'll work."

"You want me to get Botox?"

He rummages through the mess on his desk, and finds some sheet music. "Play this."

I take the music and look it over. "You want me to play right now?"

"That's what I said, didn't I?"

I take a deep breath. *Calm, Hope, calm.*

I take my guitar out of its case and set it on my lap.

I can see that the song is intended to be played fast. But it shouldn't be.

I slow it down and strip it down. I play it how I want to hear it.

Twenty seconds in, Joseph waves at me to stop. "Huh."

"Huh what?"

"Try this one. It's a ballad."

I examine the song, and again, it's all wrong. It needs a little tempo. I only manage the introduction before Joseph interrupts again. "What is this?"

I raise an eyebrow. "What do you mean?"

"Alec didn't tell me you can actually play. I thought you just copied stuff off YouTube."

"You think the daughter of Joe Cruz doesn't know how to actually play?" I ask.

He bursts out with a laugh. "What?"

"I thought Alec told you—"

"He didn't tell me you were the fucking progeny of Joe Cruz! That asshole!"

I bristle at that, but I get his point.

Joseph takes off his hat and throws it across the room. "I'm sorry, Hope. I had no idea. The fact that you're interested in Lockstep representing you…I'm honored. How many contracts have you been offered?"

I almost say none. But then I catch myself.

"I'm looking at all my options at this point," I say. "I haven't made any decisions. Obviously, Lockstep is high on my list."

"Fucking-A, we are," he says. "Let me get with the higher-ups. I'll fast-track it, and I promise you, our offer will be worth waiting for. Can you hold off on a decision until we can meet again? Say, next Monday?"

I hesitate. "That's over a week. But yes. I think I can wait until then."

"Great."

I put my guitar away, and he takes my arm and walks me out.

"I'll have a car pick you up at your house. Say Monday morning at 11? We can do lunch, I'll introduce you around. We'll make a day of it."

I nod and shake his hand. "Sounds great."

❧

I don't know whether to laugh or be pissed. Assuming the terms of the contract are decent, I'm about to be signed to Lockstep Records—all because of my father.

And God love Alec. He didn't even tell Joseph Kirshner who I was. I love him even more for that.

I get to Alec's house around eight, and I find him sitting in a corner of the couch, the room dark.

"Hey, babe," I say. "Why are you sitting in the dark?"

He laughs, but there's an edge to it. "I hadn't even noticed."

"Did something happen?"

He heaves himself to his feet and flips on a light. "You could say that."

"You're scaring me," I say. "Does it have to do with us?"

He steers me to the couch, and we both sit.

"I have to go to China."

"Okay."

"And I don't know when I'll be back."

I stare at him, and he looks away.

"That's all you're gonna tell me?" I ask.

He sighs. "That's all I know."

"Does it have to do with your grandparents?"

He stands. "I have a red eye. I'm leaving tonight."

I stand up in front of him. "You're not even gonna tell me why?"

He doesn't say anything.

"Are we talking a few days? A week? A month?" I ask.

"I don't know. Maybe a month," he finally says.

"Are you breaking up with me?" My heart is rattling in my chest, and my stomach flip-flops.

"No, but I...I don't expect you to wait."

"I thought we were stronger than this," I say. "I thought...I love you. I thought you loved me."

"That's not the issue," he says.

"Then what is the issue?" I say. "Give me something. I'll wait for you, Alec. Whatever the reason."

He blows out a loud breath. "I have to pack. I'll call you. As soon as I know more."

"So that's it."

Silence.

"Damn you." I clutch my purse to my chest and run to my car.

Chapter 23

Three days, and I don't hear from Alec.

I was so angry with him for shutting me out. So angry, that I almost broke up with him over text.

And then I was hurt—didn't I mean something important to him?

And then I was disappointed in how he handled things. I thought we had a pretty good line of communication going. I thought he was close to perfect, but he broke the love spell I had going and made me look at him without the false veneer.

And then...Martika gets a hold of me.

"This is contrary to everything you know about the guy," she tells me as I cook away my sorrow over a bubbling pot of chili. "I can't believe he'd just leave with no explanation. That doesn't sound like him."

"I guess we don't really know him," I say. "Two months isn't that long. That's the lesson here."

She shakes her head. "Sure, you don't know every little detail, but you said the L-word. He doesn't seem like the kind of guy that just tells you he loves you to get in your pants and then leaves."

"He had already gotten in my pants," I say. "He didn't have to tell me he loved me."

"Proves my point. Maybe he's a lawyer for the Chinese mafia," she says. "Maybe he's running for his life, and doesn't want to suck you in."

"The Chinese mafia?"

"That's a thing," she says. "Maybe he's a spy."

"Martika," I say, "this is not fiction. This is real life."

"Which can be stranger than fiction. Maybe he has a wife and family over in China."

I roll my eyes. "He does not have a wife in China. He has an ex-wife who..."

Martika looks at me. "Who what?"

"Maybe it has to do with her," I say. "Alec's sister said she was a mess and that she was Chinese, I mean, born in China. Maybe she went back after the divorce."

"Why don't you call Alec's sister? Maybe she knows what's going on."

"I already thought of that," I say, "but I have no way to contact her. I don't have her number. All I know is where Alec's aunt lives, and I'm not even sure I could find it again."

Martika sighs. "It's kind of weird showing up to the aunt's. And if he didn't tell you what was going on, I doubt he'd tell her. Maybe the sister, but not the aunt."

I nod. That was my feeling, too.

I dish us up two bowls of chili and plop a scoop of sour cream on each. Martika covers the top of hers with cheese, and we sit on the couch to eat.

"My vote is that you hang in there," she says, cheese dangling from her chin. "Alec's a good guy. There's a rational explanation for all of this."

"I want to believe that," I say. "But if it were something simple, like rescuing his ex-wife, or his grandparents got sick, why wouldn't he just tell me? All evidence points to either something illegal or, more likely, something wrong with our relationship. I'm just too dumb to figure out what that is."

"Have you tried calling him yet?" she asks.

I shake my head as I blow on my spoon. "I was afraid I'd say something I'd regret."

"So what are you saying?"

I shrug. "He didn't want me to have to wait. He said he'd get in touch, but he hasn't. Maybe I shouldn't wait."

"It's only been three days," she says. "Or is there something else you're not telling me?"

I pause with my spoon halfway to my mouth. "What are you talking about?"

She shrugs. "I thought you didn't have a single doubt about Alec, especially after he accepted your illness. But you seem to have a lot of doubts. That doesn't have to do with…someone else, does it?"

"Someone else?" I say. "Like who? Nick?"

"I was thinking about Matt."

I laugh. "This has nothing to do with Matt. Nothing."

"Okay, okay," she says. "Just checking."

Then I narrow my eyes at her. "How do you know Matt's been sniffing around?"

"He has? I didn't know that. I just know…he and Ben still hang out, you know that, and he's been really confused, and I just don't want his confusion to spill over on you."

I stir my chili. "It wasn't. I mean, with Alec, it was easy to fight off. Without Alec…" I shrug.

"Alec is still in the picture until he isn't," she says. "If and when he's out…this is a conversation we can have, but Matt broke your heart, Hope. I loved him like a brother, but I'll never look at him the same way again."

I nod. "But that's not really fair to him. I wasn't a saint, Martika. No, I didn't cheat, but I refused to look at all my issues and get help. I'm not saying I want to be with Matt, but he's a good guy, too. He gave up a lot to be with me, and he gave everything he had. It's not his fault I needed more."

"He could have done the honorable thing and just left," she says. "He didn't have to go the douche route and cheat."

"Maybe I went the douche route by keeping my head buried in the sand," I say. "It takes two to end a marriage."

Martika sets her empty bowl on the table, and then grabs my hand. "You learned something. You're working on yourself. And you found love again. Don't throw that away. Not yet."

I open the door wide, and he walks in.

To Be Continued…

BOOKS BY ANDREA RING

Stand-Alone Contemporary Romance

High Maintenance

Young Adult Contemporary Romance

Under Water (A Yellow Wood Series Book 1)

Breaking the Surface (A Yellow Wood Series Book 2)

Romantic Fantasy

The Go-Between (Nilaruna Cycles Book 1)

The Princess (Nilaruna Cycles Book 2)

Goddess (Nilaruna Cycles Book 3)

Science Fiction

Nervous System (The System Series Book 1)

Systematic (The System Series Book 2)

Operating System (The System Series Book 3)

Honor System (The System Series Book 4)

Systems Go (The System Series Book 5)

Note to my readers: I'm humbled and grateful that you read my work. I hope it touched you. I'd love to get to know you, hear your thoughts, and learn what makes you tick. Send me an email. Write a review on Amazon. Comment on my blog. You're the reason I write, and I'll never forget that.

Read a chapter from the next episode in
The String Serial,

Strung Out
The String Serial
Part Three

I don't know why I called my ex-husband. I don't know what I expected from him.

I didn't expect him to show up.

Matt walks in the house with the grace of an athlete and the bulk of a bad-ass. He stops two feet in front of me, and we lock gazes.

"Why did you call me?" he says, and there's not a hint of curiosity in his voice. I can tell he doesn't really care about the why. He just wants an excuse to make a move.

I edge around him and grip the back of the couch for support. "You already know."

He shakes his head. "You need a Scrabble opponent?"

I crack a smile. "I beat you 99% of the time. What fun would that be?"

"So you wanted a little fun?" His eyes seem to darken as he focuses on me and thinks about the fun.

I swallow hard. I didn't think this through.

"We haven't had fun together in a very long time," I say.

"I can fix that," he says, shifting his stance. My eyes dart down to the bulge in his jeans and quickly back up to his face. Is it my imagination, or is the bulge suddenly...bulgier?

"Why are you here?" I ask.

"You called me," he says. "You said you needed me."

I did.

My boyfriend Alec had just texted me all the way from China, telling me not to wait for him. He basically dumped me. And in that moment, with all the pain I felt, I did. I called Matt. I told him I needed him.

"I don't know what I want," I whisper.

Matt laughs. "Join the club."

"So where does that leave us?" I ask.

Matt takes a step toward me. "Are you still seeing that guy? The one you said you loved?"

I shake my head.

"Do you still love him?"

I nod.

"Fuck it," Matt says, and he crosses over to me and crushes his lips to mine.

I close my eyes. I take a deep breath, and Matt's scent—sweet sweat, his aftershave, that funny Irish soap he's used since he was a kid—fills my lungs. Matt. It's so familiar, yet at the same time, I'm a completely different person now than I was when we were married. The last time I kissed him, he was the only man I'd ever been with. The only man I'd ever loved. Now...he's not even the one occupying the most space in my heart.

Tears prick my eyes. My body is responding as though Matt is my one and only. Every cell in my body relaxes as our tongues caress and his hands rub my back. But my heart...it's torn.

I pull back, breathing hard. "Do you think this is a good idea?"

He buries his mouth just below my ear. "We both need it," he says. "Just to see."

"See what?"

He groans against my neck. "Why are you overanalyzing this?"

"Are you going to fuck me and leave?" I ask, and I force myself not to inject even a hint of disapproval in the question. It's just an honest question.

He straightens up and looks me in the eye. "Yes. Because neither of us knows what we want."

I nod. This is true.

Matt takes the nod as an invitation. Before I can blink, my jeans are around my ankles, and I'm draped forward over the arm of the couch, and Matt is fucking me hard. It feels so right, so comfortable, but the tears still spill down my cheeks, and my breath hitches in my throat, and I want to say something, something important, but the words won't come.

But I come. I come in one long, loud scream, and Matt, always the quiet one, groans softly, and then he leans forward and places a tender kiss on my shoulder blade.

"I fucking love you, Hope," he whispers.

My tears speed up, but I force myself not to let him see.

I hear the zipper as Matt fastens his jeans.

I hear the front door close as he leaves.

And I wonder what the fuck I just did.

About the Author

Andrea Ring was born and raised in Orange County, California. At age eight, she wrote an essay proclaiming she wanted to be an "auther" when she grew up. It only took her thirty years to realize her dream.

She enjoys beating her four children at Boggle, reading science fiction and fantasy, and eating bacon. She hates to exercise, but loves taking walks with her family through Old Towne Orange. She's lucky to be married to the love of her life.

She thinks every book should contain a love story.

Did we mention her love of bacon?